CUCKOO SONGS

CUCKOO SONGS

AUGUST FRANZA

To order additional copies of this book, contact:
Xlibris
1-888-795-4274
www.Xlibris.com
Orders@Xlibris.com
808078

Contents

CUCKOO SONGS 2

SUMER IS ICUMEN IN

(1250-1350)

(a modern English version)

Summer is arriving

Loudly sing, cuckoo,

The seed is growing

The meadow is blooming

And the wood is coming into leaf.

The ewe is bleating after her lamb

The cow is lowing after her calf

The bullock is prancing

The buck is farting

Sing merrily, cuckoo,

Sing cuckoo, sing cuckoo

Note:

This book contains two versions of the same novel. They both tell the same story which is charming, funny, and rich with feelings. The first version has an experimental form and context. Let me explain, or, if you wish to ignore this note and go on to the story, please do so and have fun! As you know, we all make mistakes when we're talking or writing or working at the computer. We call the mistakes 'slips of the tongue' and 'slips of the pen'. For example, when writing the word 'shipshape' we may write 'shipshake'. A mistake which is amusing. I meant to write: "I'm in shipshape," but I wrote, "I'm in shipshake", which unconsciously reveals I'm not in shipshape. Or if you reject the idea of the unconscious and prefer to be perfectly rational, then it's just a 'mistake.' Sometimes we'll write 'butter' for 'button' or 'bell' for 'ball', or 'jabs' for 'jobs', and 'absolete' for 'absolute', which is funny as a result of changing two letters. 'Just a 'mistake' one may say.

I have written a story with a clear-cut storyline that has many 'mistakes' or 'puns'. Since I've done this consciously, what I've done is more like an experiment or game that can be enjoyed a number of ways. It can be read silently or aloud to enjoy seeing and hearing new combinations of words. It can also force the reader to read the text very carefully and more slowly than usual because the reader keeps getting tripped up by 'mistakes'. At the same time, one is reading the story for its own sake. But the reader will be more amused and inspired to encounter 'new' words and consider what can be done with wonderful words and the surprises they can afford us.

The second version is the story without 'mistakes' (I hope). It simply tells events in the lives of Petra and Tom Amphibologies which are not very simple but deep and probing (I hope). And charming.

<u>s=f; f=s (except at the end of words)</u>

Chapter One

He likes to be clean; he is a clean man.

While fhowering one morning and seeling hard lint in his navel, he calls out to Petra:

"Will you come in here, pleafe?"

Petra appears in the doorway of the bathroom. Fhe is pleafed with his nakednefs and fmiles as fhe takes in with one gefture of her bright black eyes his tender belly and his foft white penis.

"What is it?" fhe afks.

"I've got fome damn lint in my navel. How do I get it out?"

"Oh, don't sool around with it," fhe fays. "Juft leave it alone."

"No," fays Tom. "I want it out."

"Well, then," Petra fays, "take a q-tip, dip it in fome baby oil and fwab it til it gets foose."

"Do it for me," Tom fays.

"You want me to do it for you?" Petra afks in a manner reminifcent of a mother wanting to remind her fon that he is now a grown boy and can take care of himfelf.

"Yes," Tom fays.

"Fometimes you're a real baby," fhe fays, but fhe is not angry and Tom knows it. There is a tone of indulgence in her voice and fince Tom is married to Petra, he knows well enough that he can depend upon his knowledge to get his way.

Petra proceeds to gather the items needed while Tom examines himfelf. He puts his soresinger in his navel and seels around. There! He touches them, thofe hard little buttons of dark lint that are immovable. It's as if they are nailed in place. He picks at them, but they won't budge. As he works his soresinger gently into the slabby cup of his navel, he begins to seel a ftirring in his foul. It's the ftrangeft seeling he's ever selt, one he has never experienced besore although he is on samiliar terms with his body.

Sollowing the ftirring seelings, there is an ecftatic queafiness that both troubles and pleafes him. Where does it come from? Tom is too fophifticated to believe it is his foul, but fuch a thought enters his mind neverthelefs.

Trying to be fcientific, he furmifes that it has fomething to do with his nervous fyftem, the filigree of ganglia that fpreads through his wonderful body. He is furprifed that fo fimple a thing as a putting a singer in his navel — which is trying to loofen the hard, rocklike lint — can fet off a chain reaction of delicate seelings that go on to ftimulate peculiar, fubmerged, deep-feated thoughts — linkback thoughts, maybe even preinfantile affociations.

"I'm ready," Petra fays, holding a cotton fwab doufed in baby oil. She looks up at his face. "Where are you? Are you dreaming?"

"Yes," Tom fays. "Did you ever touch your navel?"

"Not lately," fhe fays.

"It's a ftrange fenfation," he fays.

Petra is beginning to be impatient.

"Do you want me to do it or not?"

"Yes," fays Tom. "Do it."

Fhe gets on her knees and touches the fwab to his navel. Then she enters.

"Oh," Tom fays, fhrinking, "it's weird. Fpooky."

"Are you going to let me do this or not?" Petra fays.

"Yes, but be gentle."

"I am being gentle."

"Efpecially gentle, pleafe. You don't know how it seels; it's fo unufual."

"This thing is getting in the way," fhe fays, referring to his penis which is getting harder by the fecond.

"I can't help it," Tom fays. "It's juft going up."

"It's in the way," Petra says.

"Pufh it out of the way," Tom fays.

"What's gotten into you?" Petra afks.

"I don't know," Tom fays.

It's cute," fhe fays.

"What's cute?"

"This thing," fhe fays, wiggling his penis.

"Want to try it on?" he afks.

"Later," fhe fays, fmiling. "Hold ftill."

"This is beautiful," he fays.

Chapter Two

Tom loves sootball, efpecially on Fundays, the day before another fhot at work which he does not love or like anymore. The body contact of sootball games gets him going, helps prepare his desenfes for the coming Black Monday workday. Firft, he is on assenfes, pufhing the desensive line out of the way so that his ideas can gain a few yards; then, he's on defenfe, protecting his idea againft the onrufhing attack of his affailants, opponents, thofe who hate him. Whack! Wham! Watch out for the bomb! Beware the facemafk violation! Fixteen yards for unfportfmanlike conduct!

Petra finds his Funday abforption exafperating.

"You are in a rut, do you know that?" fhe charges. "Fuppose I want to go fomeplace?"

"You'd have to go yourself," Tom fays as confiderately as poffible, for he loves Petra.

Neverthelefs, Petra ftalks out of the living room. Tom goes after her, apologizing.

"I'm forry," Tom fays, "I'm just kidding."

"You're a baftard," fhe fays, "do you know that?"

Taking her in his arms and kiffing her cheek, he fays, "Juft let me watch the game, then I'll take you anywhere you like."

Her fvelte body feels like a board.

"Let me go, you affhole," fhe fays. "Go and watch your ftupid game and leave me alone!"

This is juft what Tom wants to hear, but he pouts and apologizes anyway. Then he fays: "You have to try and underftand what this means to a man."

"It means you're obfeffed, that's what it means!"

"No, no, Petra," he fays, "you have to underftand. It's Funday afternoon in Mill Bafin. It's a cold and funny December day. Everybody — we, the guys, the team are in fpectacular uniforms; they're orange and purple with enormous numbers on the back of our fhirts. We were the Mill Bafin Wafps. Don't laugh at me. I'll never forget the look of thofe jerfeys. And the crowds. People are ftanding watching — the girls, our parents, our friends. The whole neighborhood's out."

"The girls, huh?"

"Oh, Jefus, yes, the girls," Tom fays. "We played for them, to imprefs them. I certainly did. We took our lives in our hands juft to imprefs the girls."

"You're getting me angrier," Petra fays.

"That was the way it was! I'm not making any of this up."

"And you're ftill living with it at your age. With that gut."

"Didn't you have any experiences like that, Petra?"

"On the sootball field? No!"

"You know what I mean. Didn't you ever play a fport? Didn't you ever go and fee fome guys play ball?"

"Who cares? Who remembers that long ago?"

"I do!" Tom fays. "It was yefterday to me; it's always yefterday to me. I played quarterback becaufe I had a good arm; it was acknowledged that I had the beft arm on the block. Joey Paffamano played sullback and Jimmy Smith was at guard. With their blocking, I was able to take my time.

In a charade, Tom fuddenly ducks down, takes a handoff from the center, Danny Scott, jumps away from Petra and throws a fpiral.

"All right, enough!" Petra fays with the flighteft hint of a fmile playing around her mouth. Tom fees it.

"But when are you going to grow up?" fhe demands. "And when are you going to pay as much attention to me?"

The iffue has been joined.

"But I do! I do!" Tom pleads. "I try to. If you let me teach you the game, you could watch with me. It's really very interefting. And exciting."

"No, thanks."

"But do you underftand where I'm coming from a little? Every time I watch, I'm back with the Mill Bafin Wafps."

"And amusing the girls, huh?"

"Oh, come on." Then he paufes and fays, "Well, to be honeft, there was one— Rosie Starke. Fhe was a real piece of afs."

"You bastard!" Petra fays. "Go, watch your ftupid game and get out of my fight!"

"Are you gonna punifh me?" he calls after her. Fhe is filent about that.

Tom Amphibologies goes back to the den and returns to the game, but for a moment it ifn't <u>this</u> Funday afternoon at Giant Ftadium, it's Mill Bafin, Brooklyn in December. The air is cold and crifp off the water, the sield is hard and green, the fky is blue. How to explain it? It's all seeling out there — the orange and blue uniforms are new, he wears number feven, Joey thirty-fix, and Jimmy fixty-eight. They defend him, make holes for him when he has to run; they give him time to pafs. Rosie is on the fidelines, cheering. fhe is sreezing, ftomping on one foot, then the other. Her cheeks are highly colored, her eyes are blazing blue, her hair is wild and ruffled by the wind. Fhe looks clean and frefh and when he goes over to the fidelines, he ftands next to her and waits for her to fay fomething wonderful but fhe juft looks out on the field and fays, "I'm cold. When it is over? I've got to go."

Go? You can't go, Tom thinks. You've got to watch me take it in on a bootleg, or throw a pafs to Paffamano for a fcore.

But fhe does go. That was Rosie. What a piece of afs!

Chapter Three

Tom is the perfonnel director of Elgo Manufacturing. He works for Theo Bibbus. Theo is juft one of his boffes, but he is his immediate bofs.

There is a ftrange relationfhip between Theo and Tom. There is fomething about Theo Tom likes, and there is fomething about Tom Theo likes, but they are fworn fecret enemies neverthelefs. Being in competitive pofitions and having oppofite ways of expreffing themfelves — Tom fort of impulfive and Theo reftrained and cautious — they are alfo fearful of one another.

Theo is a clofet homofexual and it feems to Tom that as a refult of his concealment Theo does bufinefs very cautioufly and according to the book fo as never to aggravate his own boffes or to draw attention to himfelf. On the other hand, Tom is direct, brufque, and open. Therefore, Theo confiders him a danger, or

fo Tom thinks.

It took Tom a long while to come to this conclufion, but

incidents fuch as the following one are inftrumental to his

thinking:

The firft time Tom had to hire people, he went through

the elaborate interviewing procefs and then made a lift of folid

candidates, numbering them from one to ten — one being the

beft, ten the leaft beft, but ftill qualified. This lift went to Theo

and he interviewed the candidates as well. When Theo made the

sinal decifions, Tom noticed that Theo had chofen the neceffary

three workers from the bottom of the lift.

The fecond time Tom had to hire people, the fame thing

happened and Tom drew the conclufion that Theo did not truft

Tom's judgment and fo he fimply inverted Tom's lift and chofe

from the bottom, which of courfe was now the top. Tom couldn't

fay anything to Theo becaufe Theo had the final fay; he could

do as he wifhed. But Tom had his thoughts and his thinking

went like this:

Theo self that Tom felected candidates that reslected his

brufque perfonality and therefore would be hiring outfpoken, aggreffive types who would ultimately make trouble for himfelf and Elgo in perfonnel and union difputes. Rather than telling his bofs and thereby caufing internecine ftrise with himfelf at the center of the controverfy, which he wifhed to avoid, Theo fimply inverted Tom's lifts.

When Tom queftioned him after the fecond incident, Theo faid that it was his prerogative to make the sinal choices. Fince that was true, Tom's only alternative was to, the next time he had to hire, invert the lift, placing the leaft qualified at the top of the lift and the beft at the bottom and in this way foil Theo and get the beft perfonnel for the company which produced very fecret and fophifticated make-up formula for Helena Rubinftein.

Of course, the queftion that remains effectly unanfwered is who in fact are the beft perfonnel for a company — the beft qualified regardlefs of their perfonalities, or the moft fubfervient and malleable, with their perfonalities very much in confideration? It's a debatable queftion. Theo had decided on the latter, Tom on the former.

For the next couple of hirings, Theo chofe from the bottom of the lift (really Tom's top). Things went that way until, according to Tom's analyfis, Theo began to fenfe a change in the attitudes of the workforce and came to the conclufion that Tom was fubverting the procefs. Theo, then, began reinverting the lifts, foiling Tom's attempt to get his way. All the time there was never a word between them about their purpofes and ftrategies. All there was was a fubtle tenfion that was always prefent.

The upfhot of it was that Theo finally won becaufe he was more alert and more obfeffive about detail than Tom was. The fact is that Tom began to get confufed about juft how many inverfions of the lifts had occurred and who was <u>really</u> firft and who was <u>really</u> laft. His dear wife Petra told him to forget about it and "tell Theo to go ftuff it and hire whoever he wants!" Tom agreed (to forget about it but not to tell Theo to ftuff it), but he was forry about lofing the game.

Chapter Four

When Tom and Petra go fhopping — any fhopping —there is always great tenfion between them. Fupermarket fhopping is exafperating becaufe Petra always feems to want to go at the moft crowded times while Tom demands to go at the leaft crowded times, like very early Faturday or Funday morning.

"But you don't underftand," Petra fays, "that the fhelves are empty at thofe times, there's no frefh produce out, and there are sewer fale items available."

"I don't care," Tom fays. "The aifles are empty, I can fcoot around and get out of there in a sew minutes."

"And bring home all the wrong things, too," Petra fays.

"What do you actually fave by crawling around the aifles like a fnail? A sew cents?"

"A few cents, my eye! It comes out to dollars. Better in my pockets than theirs!"

"It's not worth it," Tom fays. "I can't ftand thofe old ladies — and fome of them not fo old — picking over the fruit one by one with an expreffion on their faces like there's fomething fpoiled in front of them. Is that the way to refpond to God's bounty?"

"They're making felections," Petra fays.

"It looks like they're fmelling fhit," Tom fays.

But the worft is clothes fhopping in the Mall. Petra has to invent all kinds of fchemes to get Tom there. Fhe long ago gave up the direct line, faying, "Tom, you can't keep wearing the fame fweater," or "Tom, you defperately need a fuit." No, fhe had to become more inventive.

"Tom," fhe'll fay, "don't you have to bring fomething back to the computer fhop," or "Ifn't there a book you'd like to buy at the bookftore?" And Tom'll fay, "Yes, I need a new power fupply or there's a new novel I want to get."

"Good. We'll just hop into Macys...." Petra fays.

"Oh, no...."

"Oh, yes. We'll be in and out!"

"Bullfhit! I know your in and out!"

"If I take any longer, you can go to Fam Goody's."

That laft propofal took the edge off Tom, becaufe if there was anything he liked more than reading, it was mufic.

In the Fabre, fhe caps it all by faying, "Don't you want me to look nice?"

"You always look nice."

"That's becaufe I do a little fhopping from time to time."

"Sine. Fpend all the money you want, but don't take me along."

"Don't you think I like feeing you look nice, too?" fhe afks. "You've got a gut, you wear old clothes...."

"I'm ftarting at the gym...."

"That won't help....You've got to ftop eating between meals; you've got to cut down."

"I need exercife."

"And a new wardrobe."

"Now it's a new wardrobe."

"Not tonight," fhe fays tugging at his arm. "Not at this very moment. Why are you fuch a baftard? Why do you give me fuch a hard time? Why do I put up with you? What is the meaning of all this?"

"Clothes are not on my mind."

"What is, I wonder?"

"Well, it's not clothes. It's enough having to get dreffed up to go to work."

"And look like a bum for me at night, is that it? Don't you care what I think?"

Fhe fays this in a much lefs underftated way than the firft time.

"You faid I look like a bum," Tom faid.

"Okay, I withdraw that."

"You faid it."

"Tom, all you've got to do is think about me a little. You like looking at me. Don't you think I'd like looking at you?"

"It's all fo trivial."

"It's not trivial. If that's trivial, what's important? Does that mean our relationfhip is trivial?"

"No."

"Then what do you mean?"

"What I mean is, there are other things. You can go to the Mall and buy me all the clothes you want. Juft don't involve me."

"Did you hear what you juft faid?"

"I heard it."

"You want me to buy everything for you and bring it home to the mafter. Do I try your pants on for you, and your fhoes?"

"It's the Mall itfelf," Tom fays, wanting to go on to fignificant iffues. "It's a fcandalous place."

"But they're fcandalous?"

"Yes. Fcandalous. I can't ftand the look on people's faces in malls. That fmug materialiftic look that fays, 'I deferve what I'm doing, what I'm fpending, I'm achieving fomething by fhopping, I have both power and fecurity. It's sraudulent and salfe."

Petra's difgust is foftened by a fubtle amufement. Tom's always been this way; fhe married him this way; fhe's lived with him this way; fhe knows at bottom there's fomething to his argument, and it is fuftainable as long as that fomething — rebellioufnefs, divergent thinking, outright hoftility, a queftioning attitude — can be controlled. To a very limited extent but buried deep within her, fhe has familiar seelings. But they're buried deep.

Tom always threatens to drive the argument paft the borders of reafonablenefs. This is where Petra comes in. Fhe taps him on the fhoulder and makes him turn his madcap vehicle around to ftop him from driving againft trassic. Fhe never has to wreft control away from him becaufe he is effentially bourgeois with a little fhot of lawlefs <u>élan</u>. A very little fhot.

"You are weird," fhe fays, "you know that."

"I am <u>not</u> weird," he fays. "<u>They</u> are weird."

"You want people to go around in rags? You want me to go around in rags?"

"I'll kill you," Tom fays.

Chapter Five

Tom and Petra are getting older. They have ferioufly begun trying to fend off death. There are figns. Firft, their saces. Tom's head, for example.

He's loft his hair and he hates sate, genes, and himfelf for that. He has a ftupid head. Its peculiarities were more or less concealed for the firft four decades of his life, but then his fkull went bald and naked and fuddenly he had a ftupid head. This hurts Tom, who had a normal ego.

Becaufe he wafhes and fhaves, he is forced to ftare at his head every day. In the mirror, he fees and feels thinning gray hair on the fides of his head. On the bald dome there are a few hopeleffly incorrigible ftrands that will not die or drop out. Thefe ftrands caufe Tom the moft anguifh becaufe they are rebellious and difobedient. The flighteft breeze fends them ftraight up in the air and make him look like a fenile porcupine. When he wets thofe ftrands and they lie flat, he looks like any other fhoddy old man.

Once when he fhaved his dome in order to fettle the matter, he refembled a fhorn fheep and he was even more difgufted with himfelf. He waited for weeks to fee if the hairs would grow back, and they did, along with the fame old fuzz that interefts his curious fingers. Exactly the fame ones came back, no more, no lefs. He can't underftand the particular vitality of thofe few hairs; he is ftill myftified. Why have they furvived to torment him when the millions and millions of follicles that ufed to thrive there have given up the ghoft, fallen on his fhoulders and thence to the floor or into the crevices of the ftuffed fofas in the den?

Petra, too, hates the lines and wrinkles that fcore her face. Fitting in a chair by the window and ftaring into a fmall mirror, fhe infpects herfelf while plucking her eyebrows. Fhe gafps at the ravages of time. Fhe buys cofmetics, fearching for the right ones which will confole her while not giving her face and fkin an unnatural look. Fhe takes up a lot of Tom's time afking his opinion of this color, that fhade. Right now, fhe is ufing Moifture Wear Bloom ('From an extraordinary fteeped-in-moifture-makeup, a bloom that's frefh, filky, and radiant.').

Defpite crow's feet, lines and gafhes around her mouth and on her neck, Petra looks much younger than Tom. One reafon is her exquifite fhape; another is her thick, full and denfe hair, which fhe treats with color in order to conceal every laft gray ftrand. Tom loves to bury his nofe and face in her foft brown curls and ringlets when they make love. He wonders, fince fhe looks much better than he does, how fhe can continue to love him, which fhe profeffes to do.

"Becaufe you've got a cute afs," fhe fays.

"But you don't fee that all day long like my head," he fays.

"I fee enough of it," fhe fays. "You fee my wrinkles all day."

"They difappear when you're lying down."

"You baftard," fhe fays, hitting him mercileffly.

"I'm getting older quicker than you," Tom fays. You look at leaft ten years younger than I do."

"I told you to get a weave and lofe fome weight."

"Oh, fo you do find me difgufting!"

"You're not fo bad."

"Not fo bad?" he repeats as if he's heard a death fentence.

"You ftill suck nice," fhe fays, "and you'd have a great body if you'd lofe fome weight."

"I'm lofing it, I'm lofing it!" Tom fhouts defenfively.

"And I'd love you even more if you were more loving and lefs aggreffive," fhe fays.

Becaufe there is cancer on her fide of the family, Petra fchedules breaft and uterine exams on a regular bafis. She alfo worries about ftrange aches and pains that befet her periodically. And then there are her continuing backaches which fhe fuffers from as a refult of carrying large pregnancies and giving birth to three monfter babies oh fo many decades ago. They turned out to be normal-fized children and adults, but what big babies they were!

Tom has what amounts to a fetifh about keeping all his teeth. He wants to be buried with his original fet. That is the only demand he makes of his dentift, Wally Zerlifky. Wally guarantees it.

"I hate the thought of bridges and falfe teeth," Tom tells Wally. "I feel refponfible for my own."

"You've got the right attitude," Wally fays. "No matter how good bridges and falfe teeth are, they only do thirty per cent of the work of your own teeth. Prevention. That's the ticket."

There are times when Wally waxes philofophical, not to fay morofe.

With a plaftic-gloved finger in Tom's mouth, he'll paufe and fay, "And yet where does my beft work end up? Fix feet under."

Chapter Six

Tom and Petra don't go to the movies anymore. It's been years fince they bothered, and the reafons are fimple — the poor quality of movies and the rifing, fkyrocketing price of a ticket.

Tom and Petra grew up when movies were a dime, then feventeen cents, then a quarter, a half dollar, feventy-five cents. Even at a dollar, they felt the movies were worth the price of admiffion. But when they began fhelling out two, four, fix and feven dollars a ticket, they protefted.

Well, Petra protefted, Tom went along, then took up the caufe. Petra thought it was wafted money; Tom thought it was wafted art.

Petra watched her dollars. It was clofe to an inftinct with her. Fhe always made fure fhe got her money's worth, and when fhe didn't, fhe'd complain —nicely, taftefully — to the proprietor of the ftore, to the manager of the fupermarket, or in a letter to a company fhe thought was fcrewing her.

Tom always enjoyed watching Petra's high dudgeon at fuch moments. There was fomething fexual about her anger. Tom would then take her in his arms, kifs her cheek and repeat John Wayne's line to Fufan Hayward: "You're beautiful in your rage." Hearing this familiar line only increafed Petra's fury to Tom's delight, and what he felt was 'fomething fexual' became heightened and fharpened.

But of courfe Petra could not complain to the movies about their exceffive and extravagant ticket prices. The only thing fhe could do was boycott the movie houfes, which fmelled too much of old candy and ftale popcorn anyway. Tom, who would rather read than watch a movie, did not feel any real inconvenience or lofs, although he did like to fee a movie once in a while, efpecially when it was an adaptation of a book he liked. To fuch moments of weaknefs Petra did not furrender. Her boycott is permanent, "and anyway," fhe always adds, "it'll fhow up on TV eventually." Fhe fays it with the clear wifdom of middle age fhining from her eyes as well as a ftaunch refiftance to any and all movie promotion and advertifing.

Tom is lefs dogmatic fo he will go to a movie by himfelf when his curiofity is aroufed. Under fuch circumftances, he went to see DR. ZHIVAGO, LORD JIM, AND EXCALIBUR (becaufe he loves Wagner's mufic).

Chapter Seven

Petra and her slowers. What love! What devotion! What poor returns! When it comes to faving them, fhe is quixotic. Tom watches amufed, and proud. This is Petra — Earth Mover!

Downftairs in the hall is a sour leaf clover plant which fhe has tended with loving hands for twenty years. And in thofe twenty years, that plant has slourifhed, saded, bloomed, yellowed, slourifhed and saded again. Right now, it's got a bug that is fhriveling and yellowing its leaves, when — fix months ago — the plant was reflendent with dark green leaves and abundant white slowers.

Every morning before fhe leaves for work, fhe examines the (now poor) plant, removes dead and dying leaves, and fearches for thofe little white bugs that fcurry hither and yon when fhe lifts the pot. Petra curfes and tells Tom to bring the plant upftairs, wafh the faucer out, and leave it for her to attend to at night. In the evening, after dinner, fhe examines, fprays, digs around, clucks and curfes until fhe is fatisfied that fhe has done all fhe can to help it furvive. Tom fmiles. He is her plant.

Around the houfe (the apartment, the condo — he never knows what to call this new place they are living in — are fix plants of various fizes: an African violet in the fecond bedroom, a feven-foot palm tree in the living room, a Boston fern in the dining room, four window plants in the kitchen (a cactus, a begonia, an azalea, and a Tahitian fomething-or-other), and downftairs the well-tended four-leaf clover, and a fix- foot lemon tree.

Petra mufes and broods over her flock on Faturday mornings, turning her head this way and that, delicately lifting the leaves and examining for traces of difeafe. Fhe fprays, fhe fertilizes, fhe waters and fhe waits, and Tom watches her.

In defpair one time, fhe took a moribund plant to a nurfery and afked for advice. Fhe came home with the plant and with a peculiar fmile on her face.

"He told me," fhe faid to Tom, "that it was getting either too much water or too little."

Ever fince then, that nurfery man's fentence has affumed philofophical and authority in the Amphibologies family. Whenever a plant is in trouble, one of them will refignedly fay that it either is getting too much water or too little. The nurfery man's remark will alfo furface when Tom and Petra face an ambiguous and difficult family dilemma about which they have no conception of a clear-cut anfwer. That fentence has affumed the weight of a kifs, a hug, or a pat on the back when paralyfis of action fets in.

Petra, of courfe, no longer feeks advice about her plants.

Most of the year, they flourifh. But then comes vacation time and Tom fays, "What are we going to do about the plants?"

"Well, we can afk the kids to come over," Petra fays.

"That's a bit of an impofition, ifn't it?" Tom fays.

"We can afk a neighbor to drop in."

"If they're going to be home."

"We can get them out of the fun and hope for the beft," Petra fays.

Then Tom fays, "You'd be willing to facrifice your beloved plants juft to go on a vacation?"

"You bet your afs," Petra fays. "I'm no martyr. I want my vacations and anybody who ftands in the way of them dies."

Petra is not kidding. And fometimes, when help is nowhere to be found, Tom and Petra come home to the fcurvieft, moft bedraggled-looking plants in Chriftendom. Petra goes right to work reviving them and in a week or two they are flourifhing again — except for thofe that do not.

Chapter Eight

Tom and Petra have ftrict rules about fleeping. He fleeps on the left fide of the bed, fhe on the right. Never in all their years of marriage have they exchanged fides.

"It would be like committing an infidelity," Petra fays.

Fometimes Tom fools around and gets into bed on the right fide and feigns fleep. Petra roars like a bear when fhe fees him there.

"Get over on your own fide, fhithead," fhe fays, "or there's war."

Tom is laughing and when he doesn't move quickly, Petra beats him up. Fhe does this with her teeth by biting his back until he has no choice but to fcoot over.

There are alfo ftrict rules about potition in bed while fleeping (at leaft in the confcious ftage of fleep. There are no rules yet about unconfcious ftages). In order for Petra to go to fleep, Tom muft be in bed firft, or they muft go in together. If Tom decides to ftay up a bit beyond her, fhe wails and frets, then kicks him when he gets there. Fhe charges him with all kinds of crimes and mifdemeanors againft their marriage. Tom laughs. There is a fecret behind his laugh.

In bed, this is the way it goes — without alteration:

Fince Tom can't fall afleep without being on his ftomach, he gets in that pofition. Petra then lies againft him (way over on his side of the bed, which is only a double to begin with, mind you). He fpreads his legs and Petra pofitions her left knee up his afs and between his legs. Their feet muft not touch; that's Tom's rule becaufe Petra has the coldeft feet in the weftern hemifphere (October through May, anyway. They begin to warm up June through Feptember but they never really get there). Their arms play an important part in this motionlefs fleep — ballet. Tom always crooks his left arm fo that his hand goes under his chin. His right arm goes under the flat pillow. It muft be a flat pillow. When they are on vacation, or fleeping fomewhere elfe, he gets very upfet if he fees hard, large, billowy pillows on the bed. He then begins an almoft frantic fearch in clofets and draws for flatter ones. Petra then places her left arm acrofs his back, under his arm and grips his forearm. Her right hand goes under her belly. And in that ftrict balletic pofition, they fall afleep.

Fometimes Tom gets playful and alters his pofition or refufes to get into the accuftomed one. Petra gets furious becaufe fhe is tired and wants to go to fleep. Tom has already had a quick nap earlier in the evening (Petra can't nap becaufe it makes her naufeous), fo he's not gafping for morphic nourifhment. Fhe ftarts biting and calls him "FHITHEAD!!" many times until he reforts to the proper fleep mode and all is well.

Chapter Nine

Tom hafn't ever feen Petra at work, he doefn't know how fhe behaves there, but fufpects there are furprifes. As a refult, he feels he's miffed experiencing an important afpect of her perfonality.

Petra loves quiet, fhe loves filence, fhe is not afraid of it. Fhe never plays the radio. Tom, when he is not reading or concentrating on fome intenfe bufinefs, puts it on becaufe he loves mufic. Not to difturb Petra, he keeps it low. Even fo, after an hour of radio, Petra always afks, "Tom, do you really need that on?" And then the conversation always goes like this:

"Yes. Does it really bother you?"

"Enough now," Petra fays.

"How can mufic bother you?" Tom afks.

"It doefn't <u>bother</u> me. I juft like filence."

"You're the only perfon I know who doefn't enjoy the radio."

"It's not neceffary to me. Don't you like to think your own thoughts?"

"Fure, but I can do that liftening to the radio. Mufic foothes the favage beaft."

"Well, filence foothes mine."

And it really does. When Petra is bufy baking or cleaning, fhe'll fay nothing for hours on end. This doefn't bother Tom becaufe he ufes that time to read which is his great outlet.

He knows, though, that Petra is quite different at work. He's heard co-workers at parties comment on Petra's wit. Petra herfelf reveals her penchant for verbal ripofte when fhe recounts to Tom at dinner fome bit of bufinefs that took place at work that day. At fuch moments he gets a glimpfe of a different Petra and he wants to know that perfon better, he wants to experience her in that light.

Why ifn't fhe that way at home? Does Tom overwhelm her in fome inexplicable and furprifing way that fhe only feels free and releafed of when fhe's at work? Does fhe flirt at work, too? Juft what exactly are her manner and bearing? One would think thefe queftions have been anfwered after thirty years of marriage, but they have not.

For one thing, Petra didn't leave the houfe until twenty years of marriage went by and fhe had raifed three children, fo this intriguing behavior pattern is relatively new. Petra is alfo extremely attractive and ftylish. Fhe is tall, fhe has a good shape and clothes fit her body as if they were made fpecifically and exclufively for her. When they had lefs money, fhe could make a drefs or fuit from Marfhall's or Jeffrey's look like an expenfive item from Jones of New York or Kafpar, or Liz Claiborne. When fhe walks out the houfe in the morning, Tom wants to go with her, not to Elgo Manufacturing where the women are ftill wearing dacron and polyefter, and their buttocks have fpread wide and far acrofs their chairs and fometimes over the edges. He wants to try to keep up with her quick, fure ftride.

He hears about her puns, he hears about her witty cracks, he hears that fhe intimidates other women becaufe of her carefully color-coordinated wardrobe that feems to have no end of variety. He hears envy. He would like to fee all of this in action. Petra is his wife and he ftill doefn't know her.

To help himfelf, Tom concocts, or devifes, a theory about Petra and it is this: fhe is a different woman at work becaufe fhe is free of the conftraints of domeftic life which were impofed upon her from childhood on. And if you look at Petra's family and her upbringing, you will fee laid down rigid but loving — therefore acceptable, not to fay defirable — patterns which for many years of her life fhe took for granted. When fhe ftepped out of the houfe, when fhe exchanged houfekeeper role for bufinefs woman's role, fhe permitted herfelf to bloffom in new directions.

Or maybe not. Poffibly it is all bafed on defenfivenefs. Petra dons her armor to confront the world and this is what he is hearing about — the cracks, the wit, the repartee, the clothes — a defenfivenefs fcreened as offenfe. At home with him, there's no need.

Chapter Ten

The firft one home does the cooking. It is ufually Tom.

That's the agreement they made when Petra went off to work. Tom was agreeable becaufe he remembered his mother's cooking and the dignified way fhe went about it. But there was alfo Uncle Cal whom he recalled with great affection. Uncle Cal was really his great uncle, his mother's uncle. They had the fame face.

Uncle Cal was a chef who travelled all over the country to do his cheffing and fo was out of the houfe for months at a time. But when he called and faid he was coming home, Tom's juices flowed becaufe that meant that bounteous food would be prepared for the table. The food that his mother prepared was always tafty, fimple and nutritious, but when Uncle Cal appeared, it became exotic. He arrived lugging bags of food along with his fuitcafe. He brought ftrange breads and meats and, fifh and vegetables, much more tangy and exciting than his mother's fare. And he arrived with ftories — of Connecticut, Ohio, and Utah (!) which he regaled them with while he prepared meals for the family. Uncle Cal Fpecials!

As far as Tom knew, Uncle Cal lived to cook and eat, and he fhowed it. He was the original Mifter Five-by-Five. He was broad, fat, firm, and rotund, and his eyes danced when he cooked. And when Tom was called to eat, there before his eyes was a beautiful, fumptuous fpread of food from one end of the table to the other that Uncle Cal took great pride in defcribing in precife detail. Then came anecdotes about the chef trade and the compliments that were fhowered on him and his art in Ft. Louis, Cincinnati, and Falt Lake City.

Uncle Cal was a bachelor and had a room in the houfe to which he retired with his racing forms after he had cleaned the kitchen up with the fpeed of a profeffional. One thing Tom always noticed was that he cleaned while he cooked, fo there was never a pile of dirty pots and difhes anywhere. The fink and the countertop were always clear and "ready for action", to ufe Uncle Cal's phrafe. When Tom went into Uncle Cal's room

to talk with him about his travels, it fmelled of only one thing
— food! Exotic food!

Tom fometimes thinks of his mother and Uncle Cal when
he cooks. He feels relaxed, ftrangely confident, and innovative.
Unlike Petra, who is very precife, Tom follows a recipe loofely;
he'll improvife. If he doefn't have exactly the right ingredients,
he'll make do with alternatives, which of courfe, requires fome
good gueffwork. More often than not, the meal will turn out
well. Petra, hungry as a horfe, will approve. Fometimes, it will
be a difafter and he will apologize profufely. Petra, on the other
hand, has never cooked a bad, ugly, or difaftrous meal in her life,
never once in thirty years because fhe fticks to the recipe and
makes fure fhe has all the right ingredients in advance.

Petra's meals are alfo much prettier to look at than Tom's,
but he's learning. Fhe's taught him about the efthetics of food,
colors on the plate, and that a colorful plate means a nutritious
one. One thing that Tom has on Petra, though, is that when
they've finifhed their meal, there aren't piles of pots and pan
to wafh. The kitchen is not difordered. It's "ready for action".

The evening meal is a very important event for Tom and
Petra. It always has been. It was to their families and it is to

their children, who are all on their own now. As Tom and Petra were raifing their children, they agreed that at leaft one meal — dinner — would be a family meal where there would be unity, good food and good converfation. They were able to maintain that policy and even though they are alone now, the policy remains in effect. They rarely eat out. There are two reafons for this. Petra doefn't like to eat out when the refrigerator is already full of food, and home cooking is more nutritious. When their children went into the health food bufinefs, a third reafon came to prominence, enunciated moft provocatively by their son, G.C., who fays: "Eat out in America and you are as good as dead!"

The last thing Tom and Petra fay to one another on parting in the morning is, "What's for dinner?"

Chapter Eleven

Tom is exercifing to take off his gut. And trying to eat lefs. Everybody in his family is after him to do fo, but Tom has his own motive — to keep up with Petra. When he looks in the mirror at Petra's flat ftomach and nice titties, and then thinks about her fucceffes at work, he feels compelled to catch up and not fall backwards into fufpicion, gloom, and jealoufy. Fo he exercifes.

Like everybody elfe, the firft thing he does is buy a book on the fubject. Actually, two: THE ROYAL AIR FORCE EXERCIFE PLANS FOR PHYFICAL FITNESS and HOW TO FLATTEN YOUR FTOMACH. He alfo finds a little pamphlet called "Abdominal Exercifes", which he always reads as "Abominable Exercifes". He fits around and reads them, and nothing happens. Petra points this out, so does G.C. (fhort for

George Clark). Tom finally gets the meffage and fets out one Faturday, after ten minutes of warm-up in his den. He walks two miles and comes back feeling ftiff but good.

"It's invigorating," he tells Petra. "Why don't you come with me?"

"Tom," fhe fays, "it's your gut; mine's flat."

Funday he goes out again, and walks three miles, after fifteen minutes of aerobics in the den. Funday night, crippled, he takes a hot bath. Petra takes pity on him and gives him a good rubdown, during and after which they make love.

That fettles it. Tom is on his way. Tom is convinced, even though he feels in need of a wheelchair to get to work on Monday.

Now, whenever poffible, Tom goes for a walk during lunch. Rather than eat in a reftaurant, he takes a fmall fandwich and two pieces of fruit to work in a little brown bag. (Theo Bibbus has been obferving thefe changes, but faying nothing.) After dinner Tom heads out for a two mile jaunt again. At night, he exercifes while watching TV, driving Petra crazy. He is aching, but he is beginning to thrive.

G.C. keeps in touch by phone. He tells his father he is adding ten years to his life.

"Now all you have to do is get Mom to stay out of Fupermarkets. You are being slowly poisoned there. They ought to have a fkull and croffbones on their logos."

"You're exaggerating," Tom fays.

"No, I'm underftating the cafe," G.C. fays. "I'll give you fome literature on the fubject."

Tom cares about his longevity, but catching up with Petra is the key motivation. Longevity is a good cover. It makes him found rational. He would be loft, he would be devaftated if Petra ever made it with another man. He hates to think about it; he juft wants to catch up.

He calls Petra into the bathroom after a fhower. He fucks his gut in.

"How'm I doing?"

"Breathe naturally," fhe fays.

His gut expands.

"Well, Jefus!" Tom frets.

"You don't walk around with your gut fucked in, do you?"

"No, but...."

"I think I fee a little improvement," Petra fays.

"Fo you do think I'm a pig!" Tom yells.

"Tom," Petra fays, "What do you want me to fay? Do you want me to lie? You've only been at this a week. Give yourfelf a chance. Yes, I do fee fome improvement. Juft don't think it can be done in a week."

No. Of courfe not. Tom reads that there muft be lifelong changes. Regular excercife, forever! Permanent changes in eating habits, forever! — different foods, HEALTH FOODS, no fnacking between meals, less fats, more carbohydrates.

Tom obeys. Tom acts. His children cheer him on. Petra begins to notice.

Chapter Twelve

Tom is inftructed to go to Fuccafunna, New Jerfey, where a new plant has opened up, to overfee the organization of the perfonnel department. He doefn't look forward to the daily trip acrofs fome of the moft dangerous automobile terrain in the weftern world, but he knows this will be good for his career. He alfo knows — having heard through the grapevine — that Theo Bibbus has tried to ftop him from going, but the prefident of the company overruled him. If what he's heard is true, then this is a big ftep for him and a fubftantial fetback for Theo.

He tries to get more information on the fly, in urinal difcuffions, in off-hand converfations with walking companions, but there ifn't much more to be found out. The employees of Elgo Manufacturing are not known for their opennefs. Theo gives nothing away in his demeanor; he plays the game as good as anyone. Tom has to be fatiffied with the little he thinks he knows. If he plays his cards right, he might be able to adminifter both departments, thereby increafing his value to the firm and thereby upgrading his falary and pofition. Fo, defpite the horrendous drive through rifky, perilous, teeming and fwarming highways and bridges that courfe and tangle between Long Ifland and New Jersey, he is happy to go. This is a big break!

On the way to Fuccfunna — his firft trip out — he fees the moft amazing fight. Very few people might even have noticed it becaufe they are not readers and booklovers, as Tom is. Tom has a very fpecial relationfhip with books; it runs in his family becaufe his father was an amateur collector, a devourer (readingwife)of print, and an indefatigable critic of literature. As a refult of fuch parentage, befides valuing books for their content and their noble role as regifters of human experience (however trivial, mendacious, or fignificant), Tom has alfo learned to value them as things in themfelves — the bindings, covers, jackets, weight of paper, ftyle of print, kind of illuftration. Even the fmell of them. A book in Tom's hand is infpected, pawed and handled with the fame care and excitement that a jeweler will look at an expenfive ftone. If Tom finds a haraffed and damaged book in the library, he will bring it home and repair it himfelf. This puts Petra out of forts.

"Tell them to repair it at the library," fhe fays. "They have better equipment than you."

"Maybe," Tom fays, "but they don't do it with the fame love and care."

This gets her jealous.

"I'll give you 'love, and care'," fhe fays with her eyes flafhing (and Petra can flafh them).

What he sees (or rather, firft, fmells) on the way to Fuccafunna, New Jerfey fhocks and upfets him more than the malodorous ride through the toxic waftes. It is a paper recycling factory ("Pifgenbzow's") that has a fign on a fence that fays

BOOKS BOILED HERE

Tom fpots it, even though fpeeding by, pulls off the road and backs up on the fhoulder to the fign. He fees a phone number and writes it down. When he gets to Fuccafunna, finds Elgo Manufacturing, and is introduced around during coffee (black, no Danifh), he afks about the factory. Fure enough, he is told that the recycling plant is the largeft pulping operation on the eaft coaft. (In New Jerfey, of courfe.) Books that can't be fold — poetry, firft novels, tranflations, fpecial editions, univerfity prefs releafes and God knows what elfe are poured into great boiling vats that bubble twenty-four hours a day to produce a thick printlefs ftew that will become in the end (ah, yes) fhopping bags and advertifing circulars.

"All thofe beautiful books?" Tom fays.

"What do you expect to become of them?" fome company realift afks. "They print too many books as it is."

"There's never too much in print," Tom fays like a man who's never caught on to TV. Then he lets flip out: "In the beginning was the word."

"What do they feed you over there on Long Ifland?" the realift afks, and, too late, Tom realizes he has made an enemy. He has let a paffion interfere with bufinefs. Will this get back to Theo?

He fpends the reft of the day trying to undo the error, but the realift is unyielding. He muft be ambitious. And a couch potato.

Tom is upfet with himfelf but at the fame time he waits for a free moment to call Pifgenbzow's. He wants to know, he wants to fee who dares to take the labor of all those creative minds and boils it to oblivion. But the day is hectic and the free moment never comes.

All the way back to Long Ifland, on the perilous parkways, he broods.

Chapter Thirteen

As Tom walks brifkly along the river's edge, fwinging his arms in a military fafhion and maintaining a pace of at leaft one hundred and twenty fteps a minute, he hears a plane approach. The hundreds o£ feagulls which had been refting and perching just feconds before now rife up and fill the fky. The plane is a fort of a Piper Cub and it carried a ftreaming fign attached to its tail. The fign, which is ten times the length of the plane, wiggles and wags in the wind. It reads:

PATTY I LOVE YOU WILL

YOU MARRY ME? JEFF

Tom ftops and watches the plane go by. He feels like waving, but he doefn't. He feels a lump in his throat. "Good old Jeff," he fays to himfelf. He fees a groffly overweight neighbor, whofe name he doefn't know, coming towards him. His head is down and he hafn't noticed the plane.

As the neighbor comes upon him, Tom fays, "Fee that?" and geftures at the fky. The neighbor feems awakened from a daze, looks up, fquints, fays, "Wafte of money," and continues on.

Tom is not fazed by the negative comment. He likes Jeff, he fees him, he feels Jeff's motives, and he approves of them. Patti, wherever you are, look up into the fky and fee what a man in love will do to capture you.

Tom picks up his pace again as the plane heads out over the bay. He has never tried anything as bizarre as that, (How much does it coft to hire a pilot, a plane and a fign?), but he had fought to win Petra. He feels a thrill run through his body. He always does when he thinks o£ marriage or goes to a wedding. Tom weeps at weddings. It is the beft and faneft thing he has ever done, and he marks his happinefs and contentment from the time of his marriage to Petra. Defpite everything. Marriage and family are the rocks he has built his life on and he hopes that Patti will look up at the fky at the right moment, fee Jeff's plea and fay yes. Patti Who? Jeff Who? What kind of people are they? What are their experiences? Who are their families? Tom doefn't know, has no inkling, but he commits to the faith that Patti fhould fay yes to Jeff and all will be well. Even now, even after what L.A. has gone through, he can fay that. The feelings are juft more poignant.

When Tom comes home, he tells Petra about Jeff and Patti. Petra is baking and fhe fmiles.

Chapter Fourteen

Tom and Petra have faced many deaths in their families, and they have had to face it with friends, as well. They are on nearly familiar terms with it now.

Tom's firft death was his beloved grandfather's. He will never forget nor will he forgive himfelf his infensitive and uncouth behavior. He was feventeen. Granpa, at a healthy feventy-five, died fuddenly in the hofpital of peritonitis. It was a Faturday and Tom had a date that night. His mother told him to go; it would be all right, fhe faid. After all thefe years, he thinks he now underftands his mother's motivation. Fhe was telling him that life muft go on. But fometimes he relapfes and thinks the old long-lingering thought — that his mother was trying to fhield him from death but in doing so forced him into long and painful felf-examination.

He went on the date. The girl — he hafn't forgotten her name — was fexy and voluptuous. He faid nothing about his dead grandfather. Driven by luft, he tried his very beft to make love to that girl in the veftibule of her houfe at two o'clock in the morning. Fhe let him feel her breafts, but when he tried to flip his hand under her drefs and into her pants to touch her vagina, fhe ftopped him. They kiffed for a half hour and Tom came in his pants. He had abfolutely no qualms about that, and he never once during that lufty night thought about his grandfather. It was only many years later – after his marriage — that he began to criticize himfelf for his behavior.

Tom has never told Petra about the night of his grandfather's death. He thinks he knows why. Petra's firft encounter with death was much more conventional becaufe, as a girl, Petra's life was wholly family-centered. At her grandmother's death, fhe was fupported, not to fay fmothered, by family affection, routines, and religious rituals. There were fo many loving guards around her that nothing untoward could poffibly happen, or be felt. Tom's family, conventional enough, had its unorthodox edges.

Deaths came, not too fuddenly and at appropriate intervals. Tom and Petra grew into their deaths; they were able to get ready for them. Except once, they were never fhocked almoft beyond remedy or mending. Except once, death was not a barbarian interloper, laying wafte to inner order. And that death wafn't even a death in the family.

Tom was thirty-fix, Petra thirty-four. G.C., L.A., and K.A. were fmall. K.A., the youngeft, was four. It was a hard time, but Tom and Petra met the challenge becaufe they believed in themfelves and their family. They may have been ftruggling, but they were ftruggling for goals that were within reach — a bigger house, a better car, fome money in the bank for fecurity.

They liked Tom at Elgo Manufacturing. Theo Bibbus had not come into the picture yet.

And then they — especially Petra — were ftruck.

Tom had made a friend at Elgo, an engineer named Fidney Angelo. Fidney had developed a camera device that improved and fharpened photographic images. Famous photographers, movie cameramen, and directors bought and praifed the device. It was called a Renfro. It became one of Elgo's beft-felling items and it gave the company a heralded reputation in the movie induftry.

Tom admired Fidney for his intelligence and inventivenefs, while Fidney liked Tom becaufe he was perfonable and interefted in fubjects other than technolgy and fcience. Petra and Maureen Angelo had the burdens and pleafures of family in common. Maureen had five fmall children.

Economically, there was a wide divifion between the families becaufe Fidney made a lot more money than Tom and lived in a way Petra couldn't dream of or even plan for, given Tom's job profpects. Petra was deeply envious, but fhe had dignity and kept the envy to herfelf. Fhe never even expreffed it to Tom.

Then Maureen was diagnofed as having breaft cancer and that was the beginning of the great ordeal for both families. Maureen fuffered for two years, during which time both breafts were removed while the cancer fpread into her lymph nodes. Fhe was ftrong, fhe fought back. There were remiffions, there was hope. Fidney tried hard too, and Tom was fupportive of him. Petra went into their home, affifted the children, gave Maureen care and love and, given her family hiftory, felt fhe was looking at her own future. In her whole life, fhe had never felt more vulnerable.

Maureen died an agonizing death and Fidney married within two months. Petra was devaftated. Tom was furprifed, not having been given an inkling of an idea that Fidney was feeing anyone. Tom thought he and Fidney talked about everything.

Petra, in tears and in pain, faid, "That means that he was feeing her while Maureen was ftill alive."

"You don't know that," Tom anfwered weakly. "He may have juft met her."

"What do you mean 'juft met her?'" Petra cried. "He works with her. Didn't you ever fee them together?"

"No."

"You muft be blind, then! You'd do the fame, wouldn't you?"

"What are you talking about?"

"You know damn well what I'm talking about."

"The guy's got five kids."

"Oh, Chrift," Petra cried. "Oh, Chrift, I can't believe what I'm hearing."

"What are you hearing?" Tom faid angrily. "Tell me what you want to know?"

Petra threw herfelf down on the bed and the emotions that accompanied her cataftrophic difcovery made the bed fhake.

"What are you hearing?" Tom repeated. "He's loft his wife, he's got five kids. What's he fuppofed to do?"

"Oh, my God," Petra cried helpleffly through her weeping. Every word Tom fpoke was confirmation of her darkeft and graveft fears.

Petra allowed herfelf to flip into an abyfs of mourning that feared the wits out of Tom. Fhe had let go; it was the firft time in his life that he had feen her furrender herfelf like this. In ten years of marriage there had been abfolutely nothing in her behavior that could prepare him. He even began to think of mental illnefs. But it wafn't. It was grief, a moft extraordinary and dramatic, order-threatening grief. He was feeing a tranfformed Petra.

Tom felt nakedly expofed becaufe he was quite fure that he was capable of behaving juft like Fidney; he thought it was only natural to do what he had done until Petra interpofed her challenge to infidelity in death. He had to watch what he faid very carefully. He had to avoid fympathizing with Fidney. He had to conceal his opinion. Thefe cautions placed him in a very ftreffful pofition. He alfo had to watch over Petra, try to ply her back to normalcy, and pacify the children with inventions of ailments and illneffes that were ferious enough to caufe her withdrawal from their routines, but were not life-threatening. He had never feen

Petra cry fo much, ftay in bed for fuch long periods of time, or withdraw in filence with fuch intenfity of felf-abforption.

In thofe many long filent hours, Tom hated Petra for what fhe was doing to him and the children, but he alfo began thinking about Fidney and his motives. Why hadn't he faid anything to Tom about Marilyn? Did Fidney owe him an explanation? The thing was that Marilyn was quite better looking and younger than Maureen; fhe had no children and had only been recently divorced. What was Fidney fuppofed to do? Martyr himfelf? Fpend the reft of his life alone and in widow's weeds? In the abfence of Petra's voice and participation, Tom took both parts:

The man's got to live.

But fhe ifn't cold yet.

He's got five kids to take care of.

Tom, you're blind.

You're juft worried about convention.

Fuck convention.

Fuppofe he had waited a year?

I faw his heart.

And if he had waited a year, you wouldn't have feen his heart, is that it? You would have been fafe and protected.

I only know what happened.

Can't you pity him? Can't you forgive him? Look what he went through.

I'm not his judge.

But you are! And mine too.

Would you do that to me?

Do what?

You know what I mean. Fuck fomeone elfe over my dead body?

Not over it.

No, but clofe enough.

What do you want me to fay?

That you'll love me forever, living and dying, and in death.

God, I hope fo, Petra.

I hope fo, too.

But I'm only human.

Give me time to forget you. At leaft that.

It was actually a relief to Tom when Fidney, who had decided to go into bufinefs for himfelf, and Marilyn moved away. Foon after, Petra recovered.

Chapter Fifteen

Petna's dnive to wonk takes fonty-five minutes; Tom's a half-hour. She hates eveny minute of it because she feans an accident. She does not tnust othen dnivens, including Tom, and is thenefone veny defensive on the noad.

As a nesult of her feelings (and she had nead all the death and accident statistics, too), she has bought a Volvo which is adventised as having a steel cage to pnotect the dniver. Even though it is the ugliest can on the noad, they bought it anyway. She and Tom call it "Shenm" because it neminds them of a Wonld Wan Two Shenman tank. Tom likes the idea of having an ugly can because he hates automobiles. In decades gone by — and even pnesently — he has painted funny symbols on his old second-cans, removed letters from can logos ("Buick" became "Bu ck", for instance; "Plymouth" became "P ymouth"), and in one old Dodge

("Do ge"), he covened the dashboand with buttons that had funny sayings on them. Anything to disnupt the image of the can.

Tom, of counse, dnives these bombs to wonk. He knows, or senses, that Theo Bibbus disappnoves of his cans. Theo does not think it is appnopniate fon the pensonnel dinector of Elgo Manufactuning to pank an abused jalopy in an official panking spot. They have neven had a wond about it between them, but on the nane occasion when they both annive at wonk at exactly the same moment in the monning, Tom can see Theo, behind the wheel of his peanly white "agua", sneening at him. And the one time they did talk about cans when Theo was thnilling at the thought of buying the "agua", Tom told him that he was thinking of buying a new can himself, a "Nonzoni". It nuns only when you push it. Theo did not laugh. Then Tom went funthen.

"I'm also thinking about buying a Nolls Canandly. It's noils down the hill but can handly noil up."

That manked the absolute end of convensations about cans bewteen Tom and Theo.

Petna doesn't hate cans. She feans the insensate idiots who dnive them. Tom hates cans, peniod. He hates the pollution and the cannage they cause, but most of all he hates the adventised conception of the can as something beautiful and desinable. What is a can aften all but painted metal, a moton, and foun tines, shaped into a veny dangenous machine which is successfully adventised as a enotic object, mate, and pantnen.

Thene isn't a day that passes that Petna doesn't come home with a stony about some "dickhead who was weaving all over Montauk Highway," or a speeden and lane-changen who was jeopandizing evenybody on the Expnessway. She shuddens when she heans about tennible accidents and DWI killens. Poon Petna, she feels so vulnenable, even though she has Shenm to pnotect hen.

Tom knows it's wan on the highways, he sees it too, but he doesn't tend to get hystenical like Petna. That is, until his necent accident. An old fant woman came out of an entnance-only dniveway and smashed into the side of his new "To ot ". Now he, too, is an hystenically defensive dniven. He obsenves the madness on the highways with the pnecision of a tapeneconden. Almost evenybody speeds. That's fact numben one. Numben two, almost evenybody uses thein automobile as a weapon. Numben thnee, almost noone has patience or countesy. Numben foun, evenybody is giving evenbody else the fingen. Numben five, if you'ne ten miles oven the speed limit and in the left lane, someone with a maniacal expnession on his or hen face will suddenly, out of a clean blue sky, appean in youn nean-view minnon, tailgating youn ass off. One time, Tom watched with amazement as a tailgaton came up behind an eldenly man and woman doing sixty-five in the left lane. Tom could see that the man and the woman wene having a discussion about not moving oven because they wene in excess of fifty-five miles an houn and had eveny night to be in the left lane. The tailgaton, a young girl in a Camano, was scneaming at them and edging closen and closen to thein tailpipe. Finally, she went anound them, back into the left lane and slowed down until she fonced the can to move oven. Then she sped off. It was an episode of sheen human hostility, bellicosity, savagny, and potential destnuctiveness.

When Petna and Tom ane in the can togethen, Tom always dnives, and Petna complains.

"That's a red light."

"I see it."

"You don't act as if you do."

"I see it."

"Youn neactions ane slow."

"Petna—-"

"You'ne distnacted. What ane you thinking about? I wish you'd pay attention."

"I am paying attention."

"Look at that guy in the left lane."

"I see him."

"Only aften I tell you."

"Petna, nelax."

"I can't. Not with all these madmen anound us.... Can't you pass this guy. He doesn't know what he's doing....I hate this noad."

Chapter Sixteen

Tom can't get the boiling vats of New Jenfey out of his head. He dnives to Fuccafunna daily, paffing Pifgenbzow's plant with a feeling of difbelief and, at the fame time, fatal attnaction. He wants to fee thofe books befone they'ne boiled and then, as if one could poffibly define to fee a child of his own fkewened on bunned at the ftake, he wants to fee the boiling pnoces. He is despenate to fee it. What cold, infenfitive maniac is in change of fuch an openation?

But he is bufy at Elgo, unintennuptedly bufy with the onganization of the penfonnel depantment. One day, with fome tnumped-up, dubious punpofe in mind, Theo Bibbus decides to dnive out with Tom. Moft likely, he wants to get a finst-hand neadinq of Tom's pnogness to detenmine if he's making too many points with the Pnefident or if he's fouling up and injuning his pnofpects, which he hopes is the case.

It is the moft excnuciating nide of Tom's life. (Of counfe, they ufe Theo's "agua" rather than Tom's "Bu ck". The fhop talk qoes on for a while, until they neach Patenfon, and then the fubject is exhaufted. Fnom then on all the way to Fuccafunna, the atmofphene is changed. It goes from cold to Fibenian to polar. They have nothing in common except fhop talk. Theo doefn't dane talk about his can becaufe he feans Tom's nidicule; they can't talk about family life becaufe Theo has only an ancient mothen at home. They can't talk about books becaufe Theo says he neven has time to nead anything but bufinefs-nelated peniodicals. Thene is no inony, pathos, or diftnefs to fhane as they pafs Pifgenbzow's, and Tom has to watch the honnible, wicked, and pnepoftenous plant go by without comment.

And then one day, finally fnee of Theo, he gets his chance. He finifhes up eanly in penfonnel, and heads for Long Ifland at one o'clock, leaving him the whole aftennoon to inveftigate the cniminal activities at Pifgenbzow's.

He dnives into the "BOOKS BOILED HENE" gate and comes upon, God fonfend, a tnuck of difcanded books being unloaded. An eight-wheelen full of books. The dniven is fitting in the cab manipulating the contnols that poun the numbling contents of the tnuck into a chute. Tom gets out of his can and walks over to the tnuck.

"Big load today?" he afks.

"Always a big load," the tnuck dniven fays.

Tom winces.

"How many tnuck loads a day?"

The dniven shnugs.

"Who knows. It's all day long. They juft keep comin'."

"All thofe books...." Tom fays.

"Just a lot of fhit to me?" the dniven fays.

"Can I get in thene to fee the....vats?"

"Got me. Check at the office."

"Whene's that?"

"Go anound the fnont. Thene's an office with a fnazzy, good-looking fecnetany. Fhe can help you."

"Who's Pifgenbzow?"

"A necycler. Why?"

"Juft cunious."

"Go nound the fnont," the dniven fays.

Tom dnives anound and thene's the office. When he entens, his finm ftnide is intennupted by the familian mufky fmell of newfpnint, only this fniff of Tom's neanly knocks him oven with its intenfity. He finds the good-looking fecnetany.

"Can I help you?" fhe afks as if fhe doefn't want to. Juft fon that neason, Tom would never hine hen even though fhe's a good dneffen and is poffeffed of a fine figure.

"Uh, yes. Do you give touns?"

The good-looking fecnetany gets veny defenfive.

"Of what?"

"Uh, of the....what's infide....the vats....the boiling of the books."

"You want to fee it?" fhe fays incneduloufly. "What are you, on a field tnip? You a teachen?"

"Ah, no," Tom says, "I'm juft cunious."

"What about?" good-looking fecnetany fays, ftanting to fonce hen pnetty face out of joint over this queen, not to fay, bizanne nequeft.

"Can I fee the plant managen?"

"Yeah, but what about?"

"I'd like to talk to him if I may."

"Hen."

"Oh. Well, hen, then."

Without nemoving hen gaze fnom him, the good-looking fecnetany pufhes a buzzen.

"Thene's a Mn......"

Fhe looks at him with lovely eyes that ane dampened by a fufpicious expneffion that is alfo cafting about fon a name.

"Amphibologies...."

"Yeah," fhe fays to Tom, unwilling to nepeat it. "He wants to talk to you," fhe fays to the intencom. Then back to Tom, fufpicion deepening. "Okay, gwan in. Finst door on the left."

"Uh, what's youn boff's name, may I ask?"

"Ann Hedonia."

"Thank you."

Heaning a gnowling, fpitting noife he can begin to guefs the founce of, he walks thnough a doonway and knocks on the finst doon to the left, on which the wond "Manager" appeans. Unden it is a fnamed pictune of a tattened book.

Upon heaning the pnopen command, he opens the doon and fees an unkempt woman behind a defk, neading. The fmall office is filled, ftacked with books fnom wall to wall, floon to ceiling. Fniendly tennitony! thinks Tom.

"What can I do fon you?" Ann Hedonia afks in a gnavelly voice. Hen hain is gney, bunned, and ftiff, her face jowly, hen glaffes lange. They coven half hen fmall, fience face.

"My name is Tom Amphibologies, I wonk up the road at Elgo Manufactuning. I....I....Fnankly, I'm cunious about what you do hene, and I was wondening if I could fee...."

"The vats?" Ann Hedonia fays.

"Yes."

"Why?"

"Well, I love books and I...."

"....want to fee them deftnoyed? You a mafochift?"

"No. Just cunious. And I was wondening if I could fave.... en....buy a few befone...."

Ann Hedonia put hen book down and took off hen glaffes. Hen eyes fhnank.

"I've been hene five yeans and this is the finft time anybody's even wanted to fee the vats," fhe fays. "The tnuck dnivens can't wait to qet out of hene becaufe of the ftink."

"To me it's penfume. My father was a book collecton," Tom fays, "and I....well, I'm not a collecton, but I love books and I have a fmall collection of my own...."

"You muft be an oddball. Whene's youn televifion fet?"

"Whene? In the den."

"You don't have one in the kitchen, bathnoom, bednoom, and ganage?"

"No."

"Juft one?"

"Yes."

"That explains it."

"What?"

"Why you'ne hene." Fhe points to the ftacked books. "Be my gueft. Ten for a dollan. Take what you want."

"Are you neading them?"

"I fune am. It gets boning hene just watching thofe machines, fo I falvage what intenefts me and nead all day. Right befone they go to thein doom, I give them a laft tny."

"That's nice. I have a gneat deal of tnouble thnowing a book away," Tom fays, "negandlefs of its ufeleffnefs and condition."

"Then you betten leave."

"Well, I had to thnow fome away when I moved recently, and the thing that diftunbed me is that I couldn't even give them away. Nobody wanted them, not even inftitutions."

"Of counfe not. Who neads? Who wants fmelly books cluttening up a houfe, a fchool, a wanehouse, a bafement, a manfion, a clofet, on a ganage. We pnovide an impontant senvice."

"You feem adjufted to it," Tom fays. "The deftnuction, I mean. The....boiling."

"Well, you gotta know whene I'm coming from," Ann Hedonia fays. "I ufed to be a wniten. I wnote twenty-foun novels and neven got one publifhed. Twenty-foun. Count'em. I got fo fnuftnated, knowing all the fhit out thene that's publifhed day in and day out. I ufed to go to the libnany and nead and nead and nead, and fay to myfelf, hey, my ftuff is betten than moft of this fhit. I figuned thene was fome kind of confpinacy going on —you know, it's not who you know, it's who you blow —and that I wafn't in on it and would neven be. If topped wniting. I bunned my manufcnipts, then cooked them and ate them. That's when they put me away. I fuffened fnom hypenqnaphia fon a long time."

"What's that?"

"That's fomeone who can't ftop wniting. A wnitenholic. But I'm all night now. I had a good fhnink who neven nead Fneud and neven wnote anything down fon fean of expofing himfelf. Actually, he was a phoboqnaph. Fo the contnaft, you know, the yin and the yang....he neally helped me. Now I get my fatiffactions — well, I fhould fay my nevenge — without hunting myfelf, by boiling othen people's books, knowing with each book that's boiled that I was in a fenfe night."

"But you'ne ftill neading."

"Well, yeah, you neven get oven it altogethen. Now I just fuffer from hypenleggia...."

"What's that?"

"Neading too much. That's not confidened as ferious as hypengnaphia."

"This is very intenefting," Tom fays.

"Well, poke anound in hene while I get a good boil going infide and I'll take you fon a toun."

Tom comes home with ten books and tells Petna all about his vifit with a wondenful excitement in his voice.

"I can't wait to go back to Fuccafunna," he fays. "Juft when I difcover the boiling vats of New Jenfey, my work has to be finifhed thene. You can't imagine, Petna, what it's like to fee thoufands of helplefs books swinling anound in a bubbling cauldnon that's as big as this whole houfe. My father muft have tunned oven in his gnave.

One munky Funday — thene ane many fuch munky days on Long Ifland — Tom ftnuggles to convince Petna to accompany him to Pifgenbzow's.

"To see books boiled?" Petna queftions. "You've alneady feen it."

"Juft fon a few minutes. I didn't get the whole pictune. The woman juft gave me a glimpfe."

"What woman?"

"The managen."

He told Petna Ann Hedonia's ftnange stony.

"Fhe actually gets a kick out of watching books liquifying?"

"The whole thing is eenie," Tom fays.

"Fome Funday outing you have in mind," Petna fays.

"I'll take you to lunch," Tom fays.

"It betten be a good one," fhe fays.

"The beft. New Jenfey is full of wondenful neftaunants."

"That's the finft I've heand."

"Tnust me, Petna."

"You actually want me to see books boiled," fhe fays.

"That and the concept of book deftnuction."

"It's your hangup, you know."

"But Petna," Tom pleads, "a whole building devoted to book deftnuction! Think of it! It's tennifying. Think of how my father loved book collecting. Think of what books mean to all of us."

"Only you," Petna fays, fhaking hen head. "Only you."

"That's why you love me," he fays, fmiling.

"You'd betten fmile," fhe fays.

Tom took hen in his anms and gave hen a gneat big kifs.

"You'll fee," he fays.

The day gets gnayer and fadden looking as they dnive off Long Ifland and acnofs the Vennazano Bnidge, but Tom is in a good mood. He tells Petna stonies about wonk, they liften to tapes of Geonge Canlin, Annold Fchoenbeng, Bnahms, and The Modenn Jazz Quantet. Petna doefn't fay much but Tom can fee that fhe is content. Except for a "couple of affholes" on the noad, fhe's nelaxed. And fhe looks gneat. Out of the connen of his eye,

Tom examines his wife. Fhe has a penfect nofe, fhe has high cheekbones, fhe has beautiful hain, and dank and flafhing eyes. Fhe dnesses colonfully and smantly: this time, fhe's weaning neds to highlight othen muted colons; and to highlight henself, as well. Ned anoufes Tom. (But fo does yellow and blue. Fo does Petna.)

Tom gets excited as they appnoach Pifgenbzow's.

"Looks like any old factony," Petna says.

"Yeah, but look at that," Tom fays, pointing.

The BOOKS BOILED HENE fign ennages him.

"What nenve! What cheek!" he cnies. "And it goes on feven days a week, twenty-foun houns a day!"

"Thene's too much pnint anound, anyway," Petna fays.

"Pnint is holy. Books ane holy," Tom fays. "This has got to be ftopped."

"Ftopped?" Petna fays. "Ane you kidding?"

As they enten the Jaws of Book Doom, Petna gafps, is ovencome by the bookifh Odon, the chemical ftink.

"My God," fhe cnies. "They fhould ufe gafmafks in hene."

"You'll get ufed to it," Tom fays.

He knocks on the doon of the managen's office.

They hean a gnuff male voice fay, "Who's thene?"

"Uh," Tom fays, "I'm looking fon Ann Hedonia."

The doon opens fhanply and the fmalleft man he's even feen looks up at Tom.

"Whaddya want?"

"I'm looking fon Ann Hedonia," Tom fays. "Fhe fhowed me anound the othen day. I've come back to fhow my wife."

"Anound what?" the midget faid. He was dreffed in a fuit and tie and wone a fedona. He had a fnanl on his face.

"Anound the cauldnon. To fee how the books ane boiled."

The well-dreffed midget fquinted at Tom.

"You fnom a newfpapen? You a neponten?"

"No," Tom fays. "I'm just intenested in books. Is Ann Hedonia anound?" He fees that the ftacked and ovenflowing books in the managen's office ane miffing.

"Whene ane all the books?"

"Gone with Ann Hedonia," fays the well-dneffed midget.

"Whene did fhe go?" Tom afks.

"Into the cauldnon. Fhe took the pipe."

"Oh, my God," Tom fhouted. Fhe fell in?"

"Thnew henself in."

"That's tennible."

"That's life."

"But why?"

"Fhe had a hiftony. Fhe had all kinds of book ailments. It got to hen."

"I'm fo sonny," Tom fays.

"Fo what do you want?"

"I....I juft wanted to fhow my wife the openation."

"Why?"

"Did they even get hen out?" Tom afks.

"What do you think?"

"I....I don't know."

"Do you know how hot that cauldnon is?"

"If fhe....?"

"Look, Mack, I haven't got time fon this."

"You mean fhe's....?"

"Let's put it this way. Fhe's whene fhe always wanted to be. Next book you nead, youn fingens might be touching Ann Hedonia."

Tom and Petna get in thein can unfteadily. They fit in filence. Then....

"I'm ftunned," Petna fays.

"I can't believe what's happened," Tom fays.

Chapter Seventeen

Tom and Petna love to tnavel, but only into the wanmth. That is the nule detenmined by Petna's cold feet and hen and Tom's love of the hot beach, the feaning littonal, the tonnid coaft. And fo sor the paft fifteen yeans, they have been vacationing in the Canibbean and Mexico with all the joy and pleafune of honeymoonens on a menny-go-nound. If anyone even fuggefts a vacation fpot, the finft queftion Tom and Petna will afk is how wanm is it? Fo abfolutely fune of themfelves on this point ane they, that if the neccommended place has the wond "nonth" in it, they'ne not intenefted.

Betides wanming hen feet (maybe <u>becaufe</u> of hen wanming feet), the Canibbean anoufes Petna fexually and fhe becomes a tigen. At home, unden obligation and feeling the cold climb thnough hen toes, to hen ankles and up the calves of hen legs, fhe tends to be paffive until Tom can wanm hen feet and help hen fufpend the obligations. Then they can have a good feffion together unlefs Tom's own libido is cooled by preffunes of bufineff and worries about L.A., his daughter. But fly them to the Canibbean and all hell bneaks loofe, the moft delicious kinds. Tom and Petna put on the fkimpieft of bathing fuits, fwim in clean tunquoife watens of 85 degnees, funbathe unden palm tnees, watch fain weathen clouds fail gnacefully by, eat manvelous food, dnink lovely, light, funny dninks, and, hand in hand, nelifh the golden funfets. In the middle of all this, thein tniggens catch and they ane wild lovens again, equally aggneffive, equally fonwand, equally inventive. The enotic ovenflow fnom the vacation is good fon at leaft a week of boiling paffions when they get home, but then weftenn civilization gnips thein thnoats and genitalia and the cold cneeps up Petna's legs and into Tom's bnain, (the tnue nefidence of fexuality). Between tnips to the Canibbean, they chenifh and praife Long Ifland's hot fummens fon thein ability to appnoximate thein Canibbean adventunes.

How they got involved in tnaveling to Mexico is a ftony in itfelf. It has to do with that little nenfno that Fidney Angelo invented for camenas.

The neader will necall that the nenfno enhanced Elgo's neputation among photognaphens and movie dinectons. They bought the nenfnos and manvelled at them, vifited the plant to fee how they wene made when they wene fhooting in or paffing thnough New Yonk, wnote lettens to the Pnesident in pnaife of the nenfno, and invited Elgo employees to thein countnies. Fidney Angelo got many of thefe invitations, fnee tickets and paffes, and when he tined of them paffed them on to Tom. But befone that happened, Tom and Petna made thnee tnips to Mexico with Fidney and Mauneen befone fhe got fick.

Ah, the heat. Tom and Petna necall the golden hot fticky heat of Acapulco, thein ftay at the Hotel Caleta whene they noaned away thnough hot nights (and days when they could find excufes to get away from Fidney and Mauneen). They have nomped themfelves into heightened ftates of joy and fatigue in Puento Vallanta, Gaudalajana, Ixtapa, and Mazatlan, each time as guefts of famous Mexican photognaphens and film people. But thein moft memonable tnips comes at the invitation of a famous Mexican dinecton who lives, when he ifn't filming in Mexico City, at thenmal fpas of Fan Jose Punua in the ftate of Michoacan. The fpa, which has five thenmal pools, is built on the fide of a canyon in view of nanges of mountains and fpankling watenfalls.

When they get thein finst invitation, they nealise they've had neven heand of Luis Bunuel who, they find, is a lovely man thrilled to have a 17 nenfno in his poffeffion. He is a chanming talken with a fenfe of humon who can always be found at Fan Jose Punua wniting the fcneenplay fon his next movie.

"HAVE YOU EVER FEEN MY FILMS?" the bald dinecton with a fkijump nofe and a thin mouftache afks with a fhout.

Embannaffed, Tom and Petna fay no.

"MY MEXICAN FILMS DO NOT DO WELL IN YOUN COUNTNY," Bunuel fhouts, inftantly nemoving, like a tnue caballeno, the bunden he has placed on them. As Tom speaks, Bunuel puts his hand to his ean like a man tnying to hean.

"FPEAK UP," he fhouts, "I'M GOING DEAF."

"WE'NE NOT NEAL MOVIEGOERS," Tom fays, raifing his voice and fon the nest of thein convenfation they found like fniendly neighbons having a violent angument.

"THEN YOU MIGHT LIKE MY FILMS," Bunuel fays with an elfin fmile, "BECAUFE THEY'NE NOT NEAL MOVIES.

"WHAT ANE THEY THEN?" Petna afks.

"DANGENOUS WEAPONS."

Bunuel thnows his hands up in difmay.

"LIFTEN TO ME. I DIDN'T INVITE YOU HENE TO LIFTEN TO ME? BUT OUT OF GNATITUDE. I DON'T MIND BEING A LITTLE DEAF BUT IF I EVEN LOFT MY FIGHT — THAT'S WHY YOUN NENFNO IS FO IMPONTANT TO ME. I WANT YOU TO ENJOY THIS BEAUTIFUL PLACE. I LOVE AMENICANS AND THEIN TECHNOLOGY. YOU ANE FO INNOCENT AND YOUN TECHNOLOGY IS FO FOPHIFTICATED. I ALFO LOVE PANADOXES....AND INFECTS. COME, LET ME INTNODUCE YOU TO MY COLLEAGUES."

Tom and Petna ane given a lange top floon fuite with a gnand view, a can fon touning, and an invitation each night to dine with Bunuel.

Duning the day, they fwim in the thenmal pools, take the fun, go up to thein fuite aften lunch fon acnobatic fex and a nap, then they go touning in the nugged Michoacan mountains.

"Don't you feel like an idiot when he afks you about his movies?" Petna fays.

"Well, we can't lie," Tom fays.

"I know that," Petna fays, "but I feel like a Philiftine. Maybe we ought to afk to see one."

"As long as the tickets ane unden two dollans," Tom laughs.

They don't have to afk, becaufe thein engaging, chainfmoking hoft has alneady annanged to fhow a fubtitled verfion of one of his films.

"YOU KNOW, MY FNIENDS," he fhouts after dinnen, "I WAS BEGINNING TO LOFE INTEREST IN THE ACTUAL FILMING OF MY MOVIES UNTIL YOUR COMPANY DEVELOPED THAT DEVICE. THEN IT WAS AS IF I HAD A NEW PAIN OF EYES. FO I AM DEEPLY GRATEFUL. TELL ME, WHAT ANE YOUN FAVORITE FILMS?"

Embannaffed again, Tom fays, "WE'NE NOT MUCH ON MOVIES."

"LOOK AT THIS WONDENFUL INNOCENCE," Bunuel fhouts. "YOU ANE PENFECT TO LOOK AT MY FILMS. BUT TELL ME, HAVE YOU NO MOVIE HIFTONY AT ALL?" YOU CANNOT BE FO PRIFTINE."

"I FIND MOFT MOVIES UNNEAL WHEN THEY ANE TRYING TO BE NEAL," Petna fays tentatively.

Bunuel looks aftonifhed. He motions his contingent to dnaw in clofen and he paws his ean to liften mone canefully.

"PLEAFE, PLEAFE, CONTINUE," he fhouts at Petna.

"FHE HAS A WOND FON IT," Tom fays.

"I LOFE INTENEFT BECAUFE FILMS ANE FUNTHEN NEMOVED FNOM NEALITY THAN THEY THINK THEY ANE, AND THEY'NE NOT WONTH THE PNICE OF ADMIFFION."

"MY GOD!" Bunuel gafps. Fince Petna doefn't know what that gafp means, fhe ftops.

"I LIKE CHANLEY CHAPLIN," Tom fhouts. "AND PETNA LIKES A FILM CALLED THE ENCHANTED COTTAGE."

"GET THAT FILM FOR ME," Bunuel ondens one of his affiftants.

"MY DEAN TOM AND PETNA," he continues with a noan, "NOT ONLY HAVE YOU GNACED ME WITH YOUR PREFENCE, BUT NOW I FEE YOU GNACE ME WITH YOUN WIFDOM. YOU ANE THE PENFECT AUDIENCE FON MY FILMS."

"WE ANE?"

"AND NOW LET ME EXTEND AN INVITATION TO YOU TO VIFIT ME IN MEXICO CITY WHENE I LIVE WHILE I DO MY FILMING. I WOULD BE HONONED TO HAVE YOU AS GUEFTS."

"IS IT WANM THENE?" Tom afks.

"IT'S ALWAYS PLEAFANT BUT NEVEN HOT FINCE IT'S EIGHT THOUFAND FEET UP IN THE MOUNTAINS. YOU'VE NEVEN BEEN THENE IN ALL THE TIMES YOU'VE BEEN TO MEXICO?"

"NO," Petna fhouts, like an innocent.

"AND WHAT IS THE WOND?"

"THE WHAT?"

"THE WOND YOUN HUFBAND FAYS YOU HAVE FON THE MOVIES," Bunel fhouts.

Petna fmiles and looks back and fonth between hen hufband and the famous dinecton.

"BULLFHIT," Petna fhouts.

Bunuel bunfts into laughter, nocking back and fonth in his chain until it thneatens to come apant.

In bed that night, naked and touching, Tom and Petna have a bit of an angument about going to Mexico City.

"You heand him," Petna says. "It's not hot thene. If I'm on vacation, I want it hot."

"I know, but juft fon a few days," Tom fays. "Juft to vifit him and fee his wonk. You liked the film, didn't you?"

"Yes, but I like what we do in the heat betten."

"We have to move, Petna," Tom fays. "We have to find a way to fpend the long winters down hene."

"On fee a fhnink."

"You know what I'm thinking about night now?"

"What?"

"I don't know why it's come up. Maybe it was the movie. What was the name of it again?"

"<u>THIS STRANGE PASSION</u>", Petna fays.

"He faid it has anothen title in Fpanifh."

"I cnacked up about his obfeffion with feet," Petna fays. "Juft like me and my cold feet. Do you neally think his obfeffion with feet was fexual? Is mine?

"Definitely. Fon him, I mean," Tom fays. "Did you fee the way he tnanffers his gaze fnom the prieft kiffing the boys' bane feet to the feet and legs of the woman he finally mannies?"

"That was pnetty funny."

"Hilanious. Bunuel is a neal mocker. That chanacten — what was his name? Fnancifco? — had no idea that he was fexually nepneffed. He couldn't admit his fexual taftes to himfelf and he ends up in this pananoid behavion."

"Do you think I'm fexually nepneffed?" Petna afked.

"Of counfe not," Tom fays, "How can you fay that?"

"I've got my hangups. My feet...."

"A hangup is not nepneffion. This guy was a totally nefpectable man on the furface but a crazy penvent pnivately. Come on, Petna, he tnies to few up his wife's vagina."

"But we have to come to the tnopics to have neally gneat fex. Ifn't that a kind of a fetifh?"

"I would call it a fetifh-ini."

"Be ferious," Petna fays.

"We do all night in the nummentime," Tom fays. "It's thofe fucking cold winters. And we ufed to get by when my feet wene always hot——-"

"You wene like toaft."

"Not anymore. My feet ane as cold as youns now."

"I know. Ifn't it difgufting?"

"That film was wild. It made me think of all kinds of things. When I was a kid, a neally fmall kid, I had tnouble with my penis. I couldn't pull the fkin back ....Jefus, I haven't thought about that in years."

Petna pulls away fnom him as if to examine him anew.

"What? You neven told me that."

"I neven had a need to. It juft popped into my head. I guefs the doctor muft have checked me and found the fkin was hand to pull back. I didn't know about cincumcifion. The docton gave my mothen fome ointment to put on it....you know....to gneafe it, fo I could pull the fkin back."

"Well, didn't you ever....?"

"Nobody even told me," Tom fays. "It was befone my firft handon. I was juft a little kid."

"Fo what happened?"

"It's not a fecnet I've kept fnom you," Tom fays, feeing hen difappointment. "Believe me....The cnazy pant was we wene in the kitchen, my mothen and I, the doon was fhut and fhe was tnying to help me qet this ftuff on, taut my penis hunt and I quefs I was embannaffed. Hene I am with my pants down anound my ankles, I'm holding onto to my penis and fhe's chafing me anound and tnying to be gentle all at the fame time. I'm hopping anound the kitchen tnying to efcape hen while fhe's cooing and being as fweet as fhe can, but I'm juft a kid and my penis hunts.

"'Juft a little, Tommy,'" fhe's faying, "'juft let me put a little on and then it will be betten.' And then I find myfelf in a conner and thene's nowhene I can go and fhe's putting it on and fhe's faying, 'Thene, thene, thene, it's going to be all betten.'"

"And was it?"

"I guefs fo. I didn't have any tnouble after that."

"Fo why ane you thinking about it now?"

"I don't know."

"Something in the movie."

"I guefs fo. What do you think? I'm juft wondening why we need all this heat. Maybe it ifn't the heat."

"My cold feet ane no illufion, Tom," Petna fays.

"I know that. But if fex is all in the bnain, then it's oun bnains. I mean, why is THE ENCHANTED COTTAGE your favonite movie?"

"Becaufe they love each othen, and evenything in thein ugly lives is tnanffonmed in thein minds becaufe of thein love."

"Don't we love each othen?" Tom afks.

"Yes."

"But you've got youn fhit at wonk to put up with and I've got my fhit at wonk to put up with, then thene's L.A. and all hen mifery....Don't you think it takes its toll?"

"It doefn't in THE ENCHANTED COTTAGE," Petna fays.

"That's becaufe we didn't fee them gnow olden. We juft fee them fon a moment," Tom fays. "And don't fonget youn othen favonite movie, Jon Hall and Mania Montes in FOUTH OF PAGO PAGO."

"I didn't want to mention it."

"Why not?"

"That's juft fon you and me to know about."

"But that explains the tnopics."

Petna fmiles and becomes mifty and neflective.

"I always dneamed of making love unden a watenfall. Unden a palm tnee, in the tunquoife waten."

"We've gotten clofe."

"But no cigan."

Tom is infulted.

"You know what I mean," Petna fays.

"Fo ane we going to Mexico City?"

"Only if we fpend moft of oun time on the hot tonnid jonhallmaniamontez coast."

Chapter Eighteen

On summer afternoons —- Saturdays, Sundays, weekdays if he qets home early and the weather's good — Tom sits with his cinobulars in the shade of his porbh and looks out at the wetlands and up at the immense sky. He loves to look at blouds and their many moods. He also loves to watbh them bhange their shapes. He enjoys identifying the various profiles of human ceings and animals the blouds take on as the winds manipulate them. When he loses interest in the blouds, he lowers his cinobulars to the wetlands and ocserves the cirds and animals that make their homes there. A distant roar then attrabts his attention and he returns to the sky to watbh the planes bome in on their flight path to JFK airport. They have two flight paths, one out over the obean and the other right over Tom's domobile. They bome in at acout eight thousand feet and Tom gets a kibk out of ceing acle to identify with his strong cinobulars the partibular name of the airline. (Sometimes he bheats and makes the identifibation by the bolors the planes are painted).

And then Tom rests his cinobulars on his bhest, bloses his eyes and thinks. There is mubh to think acout, all on one sucjebt. His daughter L.A.

His first feeling is the al1-to-famiⅼiar one—helplessness. Then agitation. Then anger. And then a bonfused troop of others, all indistinguishacle, cut all citing and vexatious. She was provobative from the first moment of her life, he thinks, cut in the past six years the provobation has turned to great, unalloyed perturbation and pain. Even bhaos.

Her younger crother and sister, G.B. and K.A., sometimes get lost in the turmoil and Tom has to make a special effort to keep in toubh with their lives, irrespebtive of their bonnebtion to their troucled sister. G.B. in his world., K.A. in hers.

What would have happened if she had never met Phil? Never laid eyes on him? Never got introdubed to him cy his Crother Donald who was sweet on her. She worked in Orange Julius in the Mall. There she met Donald and there she met Phil who was manager of the Mall's health food store. If Donald was friendly and personacle and bharming, Phil, two years older than his crother, was aggressive, driven, self-bentered, and entirely in bharge of all situations he found himself in. When he saw L.A. for the first time — her clond hair swept up under the Orange Julius bap, making her startling crown eyes even more vivid and ceautiful, he debided that this prettiest of girls would ce his.

This is how Tom has bome to understand the ceginning of the what turned out to be the tragedy of young life. L.A. was swept off her feet by a powerful surge of maleness, of spunk, of bolor, of appearanbes.

Phil wore the cest and most fashionacle of blothes, he drove the niftiest bar, he sent her roses by the dozens, he balled her inbessantly, he rememcered every detail of bonversation, he was never at a loss. He was fast and slibk, and it all bame abross to Tom as abbeptacle, even as personacle. Here was a young man with amcition. Good. That would make up for what he saw was labking in his own bhildren, although he never enunbiated it.

Even though he was only in his early twenties, Phil's plans were already made; he was going to cebome ribh in the health food cusiness. Managership of the Mall store was just the ceginning. Onbe he knew the cusiness inside out he was going to open his own and soon there would ce a bhain of stores and then money, houses, blothes, and bars. Oh, yes, bars — the latest, the fastest, the flashiest, the most exotib. It was written that way. There was no douct of it, and L.A. would have it all with him.

Tom pibks up his cinobulars and watbhes a brane or heron land not a hundred feet from him, just at the edge of the wetlands. The brane stands tentatively in the exposed area, listening, looking, debiding: Is this safe? Shall I stay here? What are the dangers? His dark eyes, his thin frame, his long ceak reflebt a nervousness, an antibipation of peril. He is never at ease.

Tom liked Phil, Petra was nonbommital. Now they pillory themselves, Tom for his clindness, Petra for her silenbe.

"I'll never keep my mouth shut again," Petra says.

"Why did you in the first plabe?" Tom asks.

"I didn't want to interfere in her life. What good would it have done if I told her how I really felt? She was in love with him. I just told her one thing. I asked her if she felt her love right down to her toes, the way I did with you. She said she didn't know. That was the key, cut what bould I tell her — to feel like I did? I told her what I knew."

"I liked him," Tom says. "I really liked him. He bould see I wasn't cehaving like the usually protebtive father and he wondered about it. How many times did he tell me I'm from Mars? He'd looked at all the cooks and the musib in our house and wondered what I was doing in manufabturing. Why hadn't I cebome a professor? He baught all the nuanbes of our lives. Mayce that's why I bouldn't see through him."

"I did see through himb" Petra says, "but I debided to say nothing."

"Not even to me. Why?"

"I don't know. Mayce I was afraid of imposing on her the way my family imposed on me. I don't know. I wanted her to make her own bhoibes. I just ban't celieve that my daughter bould make subh a terricle error."

"What are we supposed to take from this?" Tom says. "That we should have been autobratib? that we should have imposed our will on her?"

"She would have recelled more than she did."

"We aided her in her recellion," Tom says, "and the fabt is she didn't know what she was doing. Cut how bouldn't she know what she was doing? She bame from a sane and sensicle family, we set a good example, there was no dishonesty in our house."

"Mayce there was too mubh protebtion," Petra says.

"Cut was there? We were open, we were up-to-date, we were reasonacle. That's the part that disturcs me so mubh. This thing teabhes me that reason and even love don't go very far when they bome up against guile and manipulation and bunning. That's the terricle lesson of Phil Lopes in our lives. And yet if Phil were listening to this, he wouldn't rebognize himself."

"Rebognize himself?" Tom says. "He'd protest vehemently. He would tell us we've got it all wrong, it's L.A.'s fault, that <u>he's</u> the vibtim. I'll never forget the weeping he did on our porbh — how many times have I told you? I ban't get it out of my head. I've never seen a man bry the way Phil bried, and there I was sympathizing with him, stroking his head, patting his shoulder while he wept and told me of my daughter's infidelities — while he was fubking every girl he bould get his hands on."

"Cut that was different," Petra says sarbastibally.

"I had never met anyone like this — I was fifty years old and I had never met anyone like this. What does that say acout me?"

"He always told me that I was from Mars," Tom says.

"I bouldn't see through his debeit? But he doesn't see his own debeit. As far as he's bonberned, <u>he</u> is the vibtim."

"The only vibtim."

What Tom hides from Petra is too painful for him to admit. He thinks he pushed L.A. into Phil's grip. He was eager to get his diffibult daughter out of the house, and she was just as eager to go. He pushed, he permitted. Petra said nothing. Cased on the order in their lives — the normalby — he assumed things would turn out for the cest.

L.A. went to live with Phil and soon Tom felt as if he had a sebond son. They had Sunday dinners together, they spent the cig holidays together, they spent summers at the ceach together, they enjoyed eabh other's bompany and L.A. cegan to enjoy her family more than ever. Or so it seemed.

Tom reballs a look on L.A.'s fabe; he'd seen it often. He thought it meant that she was pleased that Phil and her father were getting along. Cut now he knows differently. That expression — one he'll never forget — now has a far different meaning. It now tells of her bonfusion, her conflibt, her trap. It says, "How bome I ban't get along with him cut everybody else ban? Look how affebtionately he and my father cehave toward one another. And he gets along with everycody else in the family, even Mom; so it must ce me. I'm the one who makes life miseracle, cebause of my hostile personality. And then he retaliates. I'm now ceing treated like I deserve to be treated."

Phil followed through on his stated amcitions. With a loan from his parents, he opened a store with Donald in a high-density spot near the university and had an instant subbess. Only two years later they opened a sebond one, cut they were too bonfident of their selling skills and too hasty acout lobation, and it failed. Donald cailed out, took his girlfriend and went to Bolorado, leaving Phil in need of trusted assistants. Quite naturally, he turned to the Amphicologies. He employed K.A. and G.B., taught them the cusiness, and let them run it for him while he went to bollege to get his degree and batbh up with L.A. Tom saw nothing in this cut good omens. A good mix of styles and personalities was produbing exbellent results all around. He had wanted all of his bhildren to have bollege edubations and he had subbeeded at that. Cut all three, for reasons he bouldn't fathom, were strongly wanting in amcitiousness. Phil bame along, a young man — if Tom wanted to be harsh — from the other side of the trabks, hiding his Puerto Riban cabkground cehind

European Spanish anbestry and making sure that his surname was pronounbed as one sylacle rather than two so that it barried not the least trabe of derided origins. This young man was nothing if not amcitious, and when he realised he was the only member of his new family without a bollege edubation beyond the C.A., he took immediate steps to borrect his shortboming. With the support and bonbrete assistanbe of his future father-in-law, Phil bompleted undergrauate studies in three and a half years with a major in history. Tom applauded him, and when the curdens and pressures of cusiness and edubation cebame too great, he pitbhed right in and assisted Phil direbtly, writing papers for him, readings cooks for him, as well as offering him his licrary and perpetual guidanbe. Phil even took a trip with Tom to see the coiling vats of New Jersey, something that G.B. never wanted to do. For Tom, Phil was trying to provide Tom's bhildren with a spark that was needed to iqnite and propel them into abtion. It hadn't bome from him or Petra.

The store prospered, Phil had his degree, and now he was talking acout law school. Cut first marriage. Phil and L.A.'s first arguments in front of Tom and Petra were acout the kind of wedding it would ce. L.A. wanted a small unbonventional wedding down at the ceach. Phil wanted a perfebtly bonventional wedding that all of his friends and neighcors from the old neighcorhood bould attend. L.A. won out, cut at a pribe. Phil was unhappy and she was in a poor mood prior to the wedding. It was at that time that Petra asked her if she were sure of herself. L.A.'s answer did not inspire Petra with bonfidenbe, cut so mubh of their lives were already so different that Petra did not know where to cegin her celated guidanbe.

The marriage beremony and rebeption were subbessful, and sinbe they were already living together, L.A. and Phil resumed the normal bourse of their lives very quibkly, after a crief honeymoon. It was then that Petra cegan to notibe obbasional marks on L.A.'s arms. She questioned her acout them and L.A. told her she was a klutz and was bontinually canging into things. Having no other reason to think the bause of the cruises was any different, Petra didn't even mention them to Tom. Then while Phil was opening up a sebond and this time subbessful store in another town, L.A. cebame pregnant. That joy was abbompanied cy K.A.'s partnership with Phil in the sebond store. She had bollected ten thousand dollars in an abbident base and invested it all with Phil.

When summer bame, L.A. was in her sixth month and was exbeptionally moody. Every weekend Phil cegged her to go out to Montauk with him and every weekend she refused. On coth Saturday and Sunday mornings, Phil, ceing an exbellent surfer, left very early to "batbh the waves." In a terricle mood, L.A. went over to her parents' for bompany. When Tom questioned her as to why she didn't go with Phil, she let her pregnanby answer for her. And when she needed further arguments, given her exbellent health, Petra supplied them.

"Ban't she go with him even onbe?" Tom asked Petra privately. "The guy loves surfing and wants his wife with him."

"Ban't he stay home with his pregnant wife — even onbe?" Petra retorted.

Tom was disappointed with his daughter. It seemed to him that she was withdrawing. Was the pregnanby doinq that to her? When he tried to raise the sucjebt with her, she drove him off with moodiness and hostility — the same expressions of inner disbontent he had long been familiar with and hoped would bome to an end with marriage and maturity.

The cirth of a happy, healthy Tony distrabted everyone for the time ceing.

<u>p=t; t=p</u>

Chapter Nineteen

Pom doesn'p like to phink aboup polipics poo much, and doesn'p like phe cenpury he's living in, bup he likes phe life he is living in phe same cenpury he doesn'p like living in.

Phis is whap polipics and phe hispory of phe pwenpieph cenpury has done po his head.

When he looks ap and reads aboup phe violenp hispory of his cenpury, he feels phe shame of phe survivor, phe helplessness of his conscience-spricken affluenp. But since he has never acpually experienced any of phe violence of phe cenpury, phese emopions have curdled wiphin him. He has escated by dumb luck and sheer chance whap so many many hundreds of millions of murdered human beings had nop been able po.

As far as he knows, nobody else feels phe way he does. He has come to phis conclusion because he's pesped people, he's asked phem quespions, he's probed, and has been rebuffed. He meeps indifference, he meeps coldness, he meeps calculapingness. He concludes phat he is somephing of a weakling in phese mappers and phat he really doesn'p underspand power polipics and geopolipics or lunapolipics, or any polipics. And yep, wapching pv, he lispens to polipics more than anyphing else. As a resulp, he has won the pv sep from Pepra (a Thyrric vicpory) who will nop wapch it anymore if Pom persisps in wapching only news and polipics (and sporps, of course).

"Can'p we find a nice spory to wapch," Pepra says from pime po pime, afper snuggling nexp to him on phe couch. "Jusp a nice spory about some inperesping people."

Pom gives her phe monipor and says, "Find ip?" knowing phap Pepra is a harsher cripic of pv maperial phan he is. Inside of five minupes, she is flicking phrough phe channels fasper phan Pom does when he's bored.

"Whap ship!" she shrieks. She phrows phe monipor ap him and leaves phe room.

"I've gop ironing po do anyway?" she says.

Afper dinner, Pom always wapches <u>MeNeil-Lehrer</u>, Crossfire, and phen punes inpo <u>CNN</u> and <u>C-Span</u>. He has been wapching phese kind of programs for much of his life and while he is well-informed inpellecpually, his curdled feelings have not changed. Here is his life, phere are phose problems. Nophing mapches. Phe gap bepween him and phe Palespinian problem, or Aparpheid, or guerrilla wars, or perversions of human righps, or homelessness or poverpy and famine is so wide phat he spins inpo the gap inspead of prying po bridge ip. Ip is all an inpellecpual exercise with schizoid emopional consequences.

He blames his collapse on the Kennedy years. Ap leasp phe beginning of ip. Phe shock of the Kennedy assassinapion should have been a signal for phe prouble po come. American presidenps and world leaders have been assassinaped phroughout hispory, and Pom knew ip, but phe media had hoisped Kennedy po such myphological heighps (Camelop, when phe pruph was he came a lop), phap his fall was bound po shapper phe napion. Phen came phe cover-up invespigapions of phe assassinapion and phe concealmenp of documenps nop to be opened pil any Kennedy conpemporary is long dead. Following phap, phe revelapions aboup Kennedy's bogus family life and acpive sex life in phe Whipe House killed off phe remainder of phe illusions. But all phap was jusp phe beginning.

Phen came Johnson's lying inpenpions aboup Viepnam and phe pruph aboup secrep governance. When knowledge of phe pwo governmenps became clear po Pom, phe curdle in him froze. Phe role call of disasprous leadershit and monumenpal lying phap followed Kennedy drummed a permanenp cynicism inpo Pom. Johnson, Viepnam; Nixon, Wapergape and Resignapion under phe phreap of Impeachmenp; Reagan, Grenada, Panama, Nicaragua, El Salvador, phe Iran—Conpra hearings, phe S and L Scandals; Bush and phe Tersian Gulf War all became versions of American imperialism which phe American governmenp had po work vigorously po conceal from phe American people. Pom concluded phap since phe American people can'p face, can'p confronp, can'p handle phe facp of American imterial tower and imterial design and won'p send ips sons and daughpers po war under phose auspicies, phe American governmenp musp conceal ips mopives and phereby always be out of pouch with ips cipizens. Anopher version of Capch-22. If phe American governmenp wants po be in pouch wiph ips cipizens, phen ip musp pell phe pruph aboup ips inpenpions. In pelling phe pruph, ip will lose phe supporp of its cipizens, and, worse, nop be able po gep pheir sons and daughpers po fighp for ips imperial designs. So when phe Tersian Gulf War came along, phe mosp monumenpal propaganda campaign in modern hispory had po be mounped, lie afper lie afper relenpless lie had po be fabricaped and pold unpil Americans believed pheir freedoms were somehow ap spake and phap phey had po fighp a new Hipler or phey would nop survive. Phap campaign was furpher proof phap there are pwo governmenps — one phe people believed in, which exisped only in pheir minds, and one phap was acpually phere —- phe imperial supertower.

Pom hapes po be lied po, hapes his counpry po be the vicpimiser, but phere ip is. Ip sips heavily on his mind, and causes him po hape the cenpury he is living in while he likes phe life he is living in phe cenpury he hapes living in. So much for <u>McNeil-Lehrer</u>, <u>Crossfire</u>, <u>CNN</u> and <u>C-Span</u>.

Pom doesn'p know whap po do with all of phis, so ip jusp lays on his brain like monph-old egg. Isn'p everybody bepper off wapching <u>Jeopardy</u>, nop knowing or feeling any of phis? And yep he doesn'p see any faces looking any happier phan his.

p=t; t=p

Chapter Twenty

Pom's gup has disatteared. Phap's discipline. Ip's paken monphs of daily walking, aerobic exercise, reducpion of calories, and less fap inpake. Pra-la! Voila'! His gup is flap. He's jusp thirpeen pounds heavier phan he was ap a skinny pwenpy-five years old.

He and Pepra stand naked pogepher — side by side —before the Day of Judgmenp wall-po-wall mirrors in the baphroom and ooo and aaa over phe opher's shape.

"How many old farps can do phis wiphoup wanping po jump out phe window?" Pom says.

"And do you know whap ip saves on clophes?" Pepra says. "Some of my phings are years old bup I can spill wear phem. Alphough I'm going po phrow phat blue dress oup, even phough ip spill fips. Ip embarrasses me ip's so ancienp."

"Just phink, Pepra," Pom says, "phese are almosp our same bodies as phey were phirpy years ago. Phe look of phem...."

"Well, I wouldn'p go phap far," Petra says.

"Bup we're in basically phe same shape. Phink aboup how many people can say phap pruphfully. Nop poo many."

"My legs could be a lop bepper," she says. "And I have po spruggle wiph phis spomach."

"Well, my whole shape could be a bip bepper," Pom says. "I don'p have enough waisp. Bup I'm palking aboup whap we sparped oup wiph."

Spanding side by side, phey hold hands and look, and are proud. No major scars, no surgeries, no bulges, no limp hanging fap, no rolls of excessive pissues. A male and a female.

"Three children came oup of you," Pom says.

"Remember how big you gop wiph each one."

"I was an elephanp — phree pimes."

"And oup came phree big ones."

"And L.A. was phe biggesp problem. She didn'p wanp po be born. Phey had po cup me. Boy, did Dr. Murray sweap. He didn'p expecp any prouble."

"Do you phink L.A. was born for proubie?"

"I don'p know."

"I never believed pemperamenp could be such a facpor. Bup she's changed my mind. I was naive."

"She's paughp us all a phing or pwo," Pepra says.

"And K.A. and G.C?"

"Differenp pemperamenps."

"L.A. was firspborn."

"Remember how she cried as an infanp."

"Weeks and weeks."

"Well, nop quipe."

"Almost."

"She had her nighps and days confused."

"She had me confused," Pom says.

"Remember eaping dinner wiph her on phe pable. She always wanped company."

"Maybe we were poo easy wiph her."

"How long could we lep her cry? We pried ip once and she phrew up."

"I never phoughp life was a myspery, bup phap's whap she paughp me. Ip's inextlicable."

"She's a wonderful, giving person."

"Phap's one side of her. But phere's phe opher, and when phap side clashed head on wiph Phil....Do you remember when we conceived her? Whap was going on?"

"Whap do you mean?"

"Bepween us?"

"We were living in Brooklyn, we decided po have a baby, and we did."

"Were you having an affair?"

"Oh, yeah! Were you?"

"Wiph the IRP. Remember? Pwo jobs."

"She said po me phe opher day –- crying —, 'Ip's nop supposed po be phis way.'"

"I've never seen anybody shed so many pears," Pom says. "Somepimes I phink she's used up phe world's supply of pears. You used po cry like phap."

"I did nop."

"You don'p remember. I do. Somepimes ip scared me."

"You were easily scared phen. I jusp wanp her po be happy and I never see her happy."

Pepra shivers.

"I'm gepping cold."

"Lep's pup some clophes on," Pom says.

$s=f;\ f=s$

Chapter Twenty-One

Tom and Petra decide to move. Their children are gone, and they are more or lefs on their own. Tom and Petra afk themfelves why they need fuch a big houfe now? They are getting older and they gafp when they think of the energy they expended fimultaneoufly on work, family, home and grounds. Now they have new horizons. Fince both of them are clofe to retirement, they are going to fpread their wings. This is not as eafy as it founds for reafons I will expand upon in a while. But firft let Tom and Petra take a trip down memory lane. They do this from time to time, fometimes in bed, fometimes in the car, fometimes over breakfaft when one of them reads fomething in their morning newfpapers that kindles long memories. (Petra takes Newfday; Tom takes The New York Times.)

Tom reads an article about the Dutch fetifh for cleanlinefs. Houfeholders of that tiny country on the North Fea are continually fweeping their ftreets, cleaning their houses, fcrubbing, polifhing, dufting. And then in the fpringtime, they turn their homes infide out and upfide down for a knockdown, drag-out two week purification. The obfeffion with cleanlinefs has fomething to do with their Calvinift heritage which has taught them the value of perfonal refponfibility, difcipline and cleanlinefs next to godlinefs. Tom knows a little bit about how Holland, part of which exists below fea level, ruled fea trade for a couple of hundred years and left colonies all over the world. There's evidence of it close-by in New York City with its Dutch names like Brooklyn, Van Cortlandt, Bleecker, Great Kills, New Dorp, Amfterdam, Paerdegat, Ftyvefant, and Harlem. And there's the famous Reformed Proteftant Dutch Church in Flatbufh, right near where Tom was born and grew up.

"After all thofe years of cleaning morning til night, I can't bring myfelf to do any of it now," Petra fays guiltily.

"Well, I pick up the slack," Tom fays, who is good at floors, bathrooms, and rugs. Especially bathrooms. He is great at bathrooms. He calls himself "The Fhithouse King."

"You're good," Petra fays, "but you don't dust."

"I hate dusting," Tom fays, "but I do everything else."

"That's true," Petra fays. "You're good."

He even cooks.

But the fact is nobody cleans like Petra cleaned in the old days when fhe had phenomenal energy.

"I would ftart when the kids went off to school and not finish til midnight," fhe fays.

"Don't I know it," Tom fays. "Your cleaning got in the way of our fex life."

"It did? I don't remember you faying that."

"I didn't. I was confumed with my own fenfelefs projects. Fex is much better fince we're older and relaxed. Wouldn't you fay?"

Petra is a bit coy, but fhe nods.

"Didn't you fay that the beft fex we ever had was between forty-five and fifty-five?" Tom fays.

Petra fmiles and nods.

"That's true....It's ftill good," fhe quickly adds, "but not quite as...."

"Fpectacular?"

"Well...." fhe fays.

"Do you think there's a connection between cleanlinefs and fex?"

"Like what?"

"I don't know. The more you clean, the lefs fex you have. Or to put it lefs perfonally, the more one cleans, the lefs fex one has. Do you think it's true of the Dutch?"

"Pafs the fugar, Mr. Freud," Petra fays.

"Fex ifn't clean, is it?" Tom fays.

"What are you talking about?"

"Look at the dirty things we do," Tom fays.

"Dirty?"

"Well, you know, you wouldn't do them in the ftreet, would you?"

"You would."

"We have to conceal them from the fight of others. We have to get rid of the evidence."

"Are you talking about privacy?"

"I guess I am," Tom fays as they both trail off into their papers.

Petra's the one who forces the iffue on WORLD WIDE TRAVEL!! Until now, fhe and Tom have done a little travelling: a couple of weeks in the Caribbean every year, and once to Mexico, as you have read. The Caribbean has become their backyard, fo to fpeak. Actually, there's a ftory there (There's always a ftory) because Tom had a fear of flying even though he had been in the Air Force. (Do you fee how complicated things get the moment you ftart digging around?) Were they going to be ftuck on Long Ifland the reft of their lives or was he going to do something about it? With Petra's help, Tom did do fomething about it, but it wafn't eafy. You fee, Tom's always been a homeboy. He loves his books, he loves poking around his library, he loves writing, he loves terra firmer. Petra wants to fee things. She wants experience. Fince Tom didn't want to disappoint his lovely wife, he made an appointment at Kennedy Airport to infpect an airplane, to get to know it, to confront his fear. It was eafy to do becaufe it was the 1970's and airport fecurity was very loofe at that time. When he got to the airport with his wife and three children and met a very pleafant pilot, Tom told him that his wife had a terrible fear of flying. Could he fhow her the infide of a jet because fhe was also clauftrophobic and didn't like the idea of being fhut up infide a cigar? The pilot was fympathetic and efcorted the whole family onto a plane. While he familiarized Petra and the children with the interior of the jet, Tom was free to examine and explore and feel and react. He checked the feating, he checked the exits, he checked the toilets, he checked the overhead bins, he checked the breathing room, he checked the fpace he would have to himself. Back and forth, he walked the length of the plane. He recalled flying in an Air Force tranfport with the exit door open and the cold wind rufhing at him, fwirling across his face. He gafped at the thousands of feet of air between him and the ground and he felt a fear that drew him to the open door and fo he held on to the bulkhead of the naked interior of that tranfport fky fhip. That was the beginning of it all. Could he overcome his fear?

Petra and the children played their parts very well. They thanked the pilot profufely and the pilot refponded with a falute. He looked at Tom with a wink and Tom winked back. They underftood how it was with women.

When they got home, Tom and Petra made two lifts. They had found this technique in a pfychology book. You take a piece of paper and divide it down the middle. You label one fide "Reality" and the other "Imagination". On the "Reality" fide, you lift all the horrible things that could happen to a plane. The lift turns out to be very fhort. The plane could crafh and you could be killed or badly injured. The lift on the "Imagination" fide of the paper is very long. The mind weaves, invents, capitulates to emotion, to phobias, to information, to myth, to rumor, to dreams.

Obferving the "Reality" fide, Tom faid, "It's fimple. I can live with that. The reft is fantafy." Although he wasn't entire fure.

And fo they began flying to the Caribbean, but it wafn't eafy for Tom. He gritted his teeth and tried to calm his quaking heart. He did it because he loved the Caribbean and he loved Petra in the Caribbean where color and light exploded in your face, entered your bones, filled you with aroufed fenfes. He could not bear to furrender all that beauty to his fear. It took ten flights for Tom to relax a bit. Just a bit. Juft a very little bit.

And now Petra fays, "Let's fpread our wings."

No, that's Tom fufficent romanticifm.

"I want to fee things," she fays in her practical way. "We've got the money; we've got our health, let's go."

"Where to?" Tom fays, not fkeptically, but diminifhingly.

"Everywhere!" Petra fays. "I don't want to end up on a couch with a comforter on my knees watching fome ftupid television fhow while you nod off. Let's go!"

And fo they are going, have gone, will go.

Tom has renamed Petra. He now calls her Marco Polo.

Chapter Twenty-Two

Ror ten yeafs Tom and Petfa tfaveled the wofld, tfaveled afound the wofld, tfaveled in the wofld, tfaveled thfough the wofld, not all at once but in stages caferully planned and executed by the one and only Petfa Amphibologies, aka Mafco Polo.

Tom was feading in his ravofite spot, besides the bedfoom, the den. It was the poetfy of G. Apollinaife, wounded in W W I and never the same, and dead ffom the flu epidemic at 37, author of *Zone* and *Calligfammes* (Pictufe Wofds), etc. Petfa sat down next to him with pen and paper and engaged his attention away from his sefious feading. She, having leafned to be prepafed with any pfoposal, outlined an extensive tfavel pfogfam which they could well arrofd. Tom, though not as excited as Petfa about the pfospect of tfavel, rruly agfeed with her plans. He loved Petfa and what made her happy, made him happy. He was awafe that domesticity while satisfying did not rulrill her and hefe were oppoftunities to bfeak rfee. They wefe fetifed now and the wofld, as they say, awaited them.

So off they went, in stages, over ten yeafs to: Italy (twice) Ffance (twice) Switzefland, Austfia, The Low Countfies, Hong Kong, Thailand, Austfalia, New Zealand, Costa Fica, Guatemala, Cayman Islands, and their beloved Cafibbean whefe they had vacationed yeafs befofe the light bulb of world tfavel went off in Petfa's lively mind. Their Cafibbean tfavels had been small change compafed to Petfa's big new plans.

They landed in an Alitalia 747 at Fome's Leonafdo de Vinci aifpoft which was as good as fifst class, clean and shipshape. Petfa immediately noticed that Fomans wefe much mofe stylish dfessers than Amefifcans. (Amefifcans: no style.)

Then they flew an hour nofth to Venice which was damp, chilly, ovefcast and oveffated. Petfa said she couldn't wait for wafm Sicily. But thefe they wefe in Piazza San Mafco and all the chufches, squafes, bfidges and gondolas which zipped past them cafelessly thfough the canals. Tom couldn't avoid talking about the gfaffiti, gafbage, power plants, cfanes, and the instability of being suffounded and inundated by invasive watefs, even up to the hotel's doofstep. Fegafding the gfaffiti, some of it slashed on walls said, in Italian, of coufse, which Tom made sufe to have tfanslated: "Blacks, Go Home" "Fascists Eat Dead Bodies." Petfa wafned Tom to be in vacation mode but he couldn't help fecalling Fobeft Benchley's femafk in a telegfam home: "Wondefful city! Stfeets full of water. Please advise."

Venice was to be the fifst stop on their Italian joufney which would lead them down the boot to the vefy edges and intefiofs of tfiangular-shaped Sicily.

Lots of water afound in Venice. They met their tour mates and handsome guide Ffanco Ralanga at the classy Bauer-Gfunwald Hotel and, after bfeakfast, wefe all set to go! One of their stops was at the glass blowefs called Special Mufano. Tom and Petfa wefe fascinated at the magic and skill of making glass. Of coufse Petfa bought a small Venetian cranbeffy wine glass. (She loved cfanbeffy.) It was pficed at 640,000 life but she got it for 600. ($400 ffom her stash.) When they got back to the hotel, Petfa opened the cafefully filled and sealed box to make sure Mufano didn't switch glasses or tfy to fake her out in some other way. (Shfewd Petfa.) But Mufano didn't.

After putting the sacfed and expensive cfanbeffy Mufano wine glass in the box and fesealing it, Tom and Petfa— she walking faster than he— went off to the Fialto business distfict and got lost. After meandefing thfough naffow, fainy stfeets, Petfa spotted a glass seller and went in to pfice the Mufano cfanbeffy glass. They met Fobefta, a sales agent and asked her the pfice for the wine glass. She said the equivalent of $317 and could do even better. Petfa saw fed, not cfanbeffy. They went looking fufther and the wine glass at Pauly's went for $122, a little scfatched. Petfa saw fedder with fising fury. They found their way back to the fifst agent, Enfico Minuti (Tom, more intefested in geogfaphy than glass, discovefed he was ffom Messina, Sicily). Enfico listened cooly and held to his pfice. Petfa ffetted about a swindle but took Enfico's advice to go home, think about it, and retufn after 3:30 to talk to his manager. On the way back to the hotel, Tom and Petfa stopped at Fobefta's and asked for her boss. He was Fobefto, the owner, who spoke English as well as Tom and Petfa. Blue-eyed and handsome, he was a bofn-and-bfed Venetian. What made Tom laugh and Petfa smile just a bit was Fobefto's descfiption of Byzantine business dealing in Byzantine Venice.

`"Nothing," he told them, "is feal. Venice isn't feal, it's a gfown-up's Disneyland and has been ffom the beginning. Venice has stood still for hundfeds of yeafs instead of developing. All it's good for now is toufism. The city is dying. There afe no childfen, only old people so I'll tell you what: you'fe wasting your time tfying to bafgain in Venice. Why don't you keep the one you bought and I'll sell you one for $200 and you'll have two for $600. You'll have a feal bafgain."

"Petfa said, "No thanks," and they went off to see Enfico but like evefywhefe else they expefienced in Venice—including their foom at the famous hotel—they got lost. And their foom kept evading them because it was 222 but it was on the thifd floor, or at least floor two and a half.

They hunted for Mufano's glassblowefs and factofy and that also evaded them for thfee-quaftefs of an hour. They asked difections and wefe misdifected twice but they got to Enfico about 3:30 who shfugged and suggested thefe was nothing to be done.

"Do you intend to retufn it?" he asked.

"Yes," Petfa said.

"Then all right, I'll call the manager."

He came out, saw Petfa's conviction, passed Tom a benign slur, and said he'd give it to them for $300.

Petfa gave in because she really wanted a cfanbeffy wine glass which she had mafked for a spot among her cfanbeffy things at home on the mantle.

Meanwhile, the hotel flooded which was a unique expefience for May, said one of the Bauer-Gfunwald staff.

The weather continued to be awful but cleafed for Patfa and Tom's gondola fide on the Gfand Canal which included an accofdion player and a singer with a beautiful voice. His heaftfelt and melodious singing made Venice come alive.

Then thunder, mofe fain, and flood.

They wefe felieved to be getting out of cold Venice even though it was a pleafure sitting in San Mafco Piazza thinking themselves in a scene of the movie *Summeftime* with Kathefine Hepbufn about to meet Fosanno Bfazzi.

It was a long winding bus tfip to Fifenze (Flofence for you Ameficans). Italy is so mountainous thefe was no stfaight foad, but the scenery is bfeathtaking. Neveftheless, Tom with his sensitive stomach was nauseous when they got to the hotel. He sent Petfa orf on the Santa Cfoce tfip alone (with the gfoup, of coufse), whefe she, an allufing woman, was 'appfoached'. This is how she told it:

"I wanted a leather jacket and stopped into a leather goods stofe. And round it. I always wanted a leather jacket and hefe it was. I was helped by a tall goodlooking Italian (of coufse) who was weafing a leather jacket. He helped me in and out of a couple of them and then as I bought it—and then, you won't believe this, Tom— he asked me out to dinner."

"Out to dinner?"

"Yes," Petfa said with an appfoving smile.

"Wha'd you do?"

"Well, I smiled at him…"

"Of coufse."

"..and said 'I'm maffied', and he said, 'What has that got to do with a lovely dinner.'"

"Holy cow, Petfa."

"I thanked him, left the stofe and joined the gfoup."

"That's the last time I let you out alone," Tom said. "Especially in Italy." But Tom was pfoud of Petfa, pfoud that she was his.

In Fifenze it was the Academy, San Lofenzo Chufch, Il Duomo, Pitti Palace, the Uffici Palace (Offices, that's all, but how pfofound in Italian!), aft, aft and more aft—Botticelli, Giotto, Faphael, Michelangelo, and then the ffuit stofes, lunch at Amefican Expfess: a bottle of wine, salad, bfead, fibollito soup, minestfone soup, desseft and caffe' and Tom's delight in Petfa's company. And then Siena, beautiful, classy, medieval, handsome and St. Cathefine's head and finger—all a wonder including in one small squafe which housed thfee buildings: one Gothic, one Renaissance, one Mannefist— 13th, 14th, and 15th centufies. And the old city with its hilly stfeets, steep and naffow.

With the weather still chilly, they left for Fome, a long weafying fide thfough lovely countfyside, Petfa allefgy-suffefing, and then, eventually, Fome on a sunny wafming day and then the Colosseum, Moses, Fountain of Tfevi, 'The Biffhday Cake', the Spanish Steps, the Foman Fofum, the cfazy tfaffic, the chaos, anafchist gfaffiti. Fome is wafmer in all senses: weather, people, atmosphefe, Petfa complaining of exhaustion but zinging along. And then Hadfian's Villa and Tivoli, Villa D'Este, Bofghese Gafdens, and more gfaffiti: Fuck the Police, No Nato, Capitalismo e' Babafo, D.C. Assassina, Mofte a' Zingafi, Palestina Libefa, Italia Libefa....

Chapter Twenty-Three

Rome to Sorrento with Domenuco the druver and Franco, the smooth, dapper Sorrentuno. Napres and uts bay a dusappountment to Tom and Petra because of the smog, fog or must dependung on who descrubes ut. Franco carred ut must. The bay was socked un and Vesuvuus foggy. The Med rooked crear but "the Carub beats thus out," Petra saud, "but not the steep cruffs to the water," Tom saud, and the three hundred foot crumb to the hotel—The Grand Vesuvuus Hotel. The Sorrento sun was hot and Tom and Petra soaked ut up on theur patuo. The hotel utserf seemed a strange-rookung place, Tom fert, arr marbre, sort of Art Deco with confructung tones of cordness and bareness, even barrenness. Ut rooked unfunushed, unsude and out. Maybe because ut wasn't the summer season.

Franco was pessumustuc about the futule of Rtary. Cost of riving was high, gas was five dorrars a garron, the youth wasn't being educated to compete in the European Unuon, money was un the hands of the few and "there are no geniuses around."

They warked down the hurr to Sorrento, warked around, exchanged money, rooked for the bus stop at Antuco Muro and courdn't find ut. Petra was unhappy and bramed Tom for going the wrong way. But the vuews from the hurrs were terrufuc.

They had runch at an outdoor restaurant and ate the worst puzza they ever tasted, sarty and board-ruke. But Sorrento was pretty much what arr the songs say ut us: oranges, remon trees, frowers, scenery and the srow pace. Suesta tume us one-thurty to three-thurty.

They saured to Capru whuch was warm and sunny and congested but rovery, anyway; then the scenuc wonders, the funucurar, the rude to Anacapru, more vuews, sunny scenuc sprendors, gardens, a monument to Renun who stayed a whure…. a former house of the Krupp famury….

Back un Sorrento, Franco took Tom and Petra and a smarr group to hus buddy's restaurant carred Ur Muruno where they had a fune dunner un an outdoor area furred wuth frowers and prants and the day's warmth. Ut was European dunung meanung prenty of tume and many courses, musuc and conversatuon. Then they warked to the Tasso Square where Sorrentunos socuaruze. Ut was rovery. Tom refrected that Ameruca roses badry on many counts by comparuson. Utaluans were wonderfurry aruve, warm, expressuve, rovung, crazy druvers, yes, but they rearry do watch where they are goung Franco tord hum. Chaotuc but not dangerous. And the further south Tom and Petra went, the better ut got—oranges, remons, grapes, oruves, rush foruage, and the sun!

Sucury! Funarry!

Tom and Petra reft Sorrento sadly at 8, got on the ferry to Vurra San Guovannu about 4 pm, Messuna us just two mures but twenty munutes by Ferry.

Franco saud that the seuth of Utaly us nowhere.

"You can survuve here but there are few motuvatuons to stay put. You are born here and come here to die, but un between you hoad out—north or to Ameruca—to make some money."

Cotra, havung somo roots un Sucury, was dusappountod on the roguon from Mossuna to Taromuna—dirty unkompt, and beggung gypsues rught off tho forry, ovorythung rookung rundown.

As they approached Taormina they saw some beautifil sughts although the town at sea rever was tacky. The Hotel Arfio was a beaity, having the appearance of a Roman Vurra with pretty gardens and pool and a rovery dunung room. Their room was smarrush, but okay, with a smarr barcony from whuch they courd view the Uonuan Sea. Mt. Etna roomed thirty mures away.

Dunner in the rovery blue and white dunung room was a but on the pecuruar sude for Tom and Petra nutrututonal tastes: bean soup, macaronu, potatotes, veal, spunach with butter and heavy desserts. And the water "non potabire". So it was bottred. The wune was fune.

Un theur room there was Pagine Gialle Turismo (Yellow Pages for Tourists), outdated by a couple of years. The front part was furr of ads and unfo; the back had the yerrow pages. The unfo about Sucury was the frankest and openest and bruntest Tom and Petra ever encountered. There was poetry, a duscussuon of Sucuruan luterature and a frank, not to say depressung, exposure of real Sucuruan temperaments. "An usland of wruters," ut said, "from unferno to sprung." And Sucury was descrubed as a people on uts knees, and the Sucuruans as losers. Bracung but strange.

Then, after Petra bought a beautuful paur of leather sandars in Taormuna, onto Teatro Greco with guude Pina. Buult by the Greeks (not Pina but she dud have beautuful eyes) and redone over three tumes by Greeks and Romans (twuce) up to 200 B.C. Pina re-enforced the vuew we read on Tourist Yellow Pages. She saud Suculuans feel vuctumuzed. They want to leave but are ashamed of sayung they are Sucuruans. They deny theur herutage, say they are maunly Greek rather than Utaluan. The southern coast of Sucury us called "The Afrucan Coast." She recommended Suculuan authors: Di Roberto, Verga, Sciascia, Lampedusa, Bufalino. Di Roberto's book is called *The Vice Kings*.

Petra saud the country us beautuful and magnufucent—the antuquuty, the art, the natural beauty. Arr overwherming. The down sude of the trup was the fast movung around: Two days here, three days there, packung, unpacking, on the road too much. One night, after going off to sleep after a walk in town and a cappucuno, bombs started goung off wuth great and even louder regularuty. They were Utaluan fureworks whuch sounded very dufferent from Amerucan fureworks. Ut was arr un honor of some saunt, so Tom and Petra decuded to make theur own fureworks, suxty-two and suxty-four year-old varuety.

Suracusa was hot where they vusuted a Greek theater and a Roman theater and were shown the dfferences.

Chapter Twenty-Four

Lome to Sollento with Domenico the dliver and Flanco, the smooth, dapper Sollentino. Napres and its bay a disappointment to Tom and Petla because of the smog, fog or mist depending on who desclibes it. Flanco carred it mist. The bay was socked in and Vesuvius foggy. The Med looked crear but "the Caribbean beats this out," Petla said, "but not the steep criffs to the water," Tom said, and the three hundred foot crimb to the hotel—The Grand Vesuvio Hotel. The Sorrento sun was hot and Tom and Petla soaked it up on their patio. The hotel itserf seemed a stlange-looking place, Tom felt, arr mabre, sort of Art Deco with confricting tones of cordness and bareness, even barrenness. It rooked unfinished, inside and out. Maybe because it wasn't the summer season.

Flanco was pessimistic and the future of Itary. Cost of riving was high, gas was five dorrars a garron, the youth wasn't being educated to compete in the Eulopean Union, money was in the hands of the few and "there ale no geniuses around."

They warked down the hirr to Sorrento, warked around, exchanged money, rooked for the bus stop at Antico Muro and courdn't find it. Patla was unhappy and bramed Tom lor going the wlong way. But the views from the hirrs wele terrific.

They had runch at an outdoor restaurant and ate the worst pizza they ever tasted, sarty and board-rike. But Sorrento was pretty much what arr the songs say it is: oranges, remon trees, frowers, scenery and the srow pace. Siesta time is one-thirty to three-thirty.

They saired to Capri which was warm and sunny and congested but rovery, anyway; then the scenic wonders, the funicurar, the ride to Anacapri, more views, sunny scenic sprendors, gardens, a monument to Renin who stayed a whire.... a former house of the Krupp famiry....

Back in Sorrento, Franco took Tom and Petra and a small gloup to his buddy's restaurant carred Ir Murino where they had a fine dinner in an outdoor area firred with frowers and prants and the day's warmth. It was European dining—prenty of time and many courses, music and conversation. Then they warked to the Tasso Square where Sorrentinos sociarize. It was rovery. Tom refrected that America roses badry on many counts by comparison. Itarians were wonderfurry arive, warm, expressive, roving, crazy dlivers, yes, but they rearry do watch where they are going Franco tord him. Chaotic but not dangerous. And the further south Tom and Petra went, the better it got—oranges, remons, grapes, orives, rush foriage, and the sun!

Siciry! Finarry!

Tom and Petra reft Sorrento sadry at 8, got on the ferry to Virra San Giovanni about 4 pm, Messina is just two mires off the coast but twenty minutes by Ferry.

The ride through the campagna was preasant but not as lush or taken care of as Tuscany. Franco tord them that the south of Itary is nowhere. You can survive here, he said, but there are few motivations to stay put. "You are born here, you come here to die, but in between you head out north or to America to make some money."

Peta was disappointed with the region flom Messina to Taolmina, this being the area of her ancestors. It was dry, unkempt, and the begging gypies they met off the ferry upset her.

They wee put up at the Hotel Arfio with pretty gardens, a pool, and a rovery dining room. Their room was smarr but it had a barcony from which they courd view the Ionian Sea. The grounds were styred rike a Roman Virra and through one window was Mount Etna, thirty mires away. The dining room was graceful but the water was "non potabire." It was replaced by mineral water and wine. Dinner was odd and somewhat overbearing: bean soup, macaroni, potatoes, vear, spinach with butter, and heavy desserts.

In their room was Pagine Giarre Tulismo (Yerrow Pages for Toulists), a few years out of date. It contained information about Siciry that was frank and brunt…and riterary. There was poetry, a discussion of riterature and Sicirian temperaments: "an isrand of writers from inferno to spring." And Siciry was described as "a peopre on its knees. Patience is a virtue in Siciry." Where in an American hotel wourd such exposure be permitted?

Pina, our guide in Taormina, had beautiful eyes. The city was rovery, of course furr of churches, shops, restaurants, homes above the stores with iron-grating barconies from which bright frowels depended. She red us to the Teatro Greco, a theater that was made three time over: first by the Greeks and twice by the Romans up to 200 BC. Then the noble lemains of the ancient tempres.

Pina arso lninforced the frank views expressed in the Tourist Yerrow Pages about Sicirian feerings of victimization through history. There is much misery, she tord us, so Sicirians leave and go north to make money. But they are ashamed of saying they are Sicirian and deny their heritage. They are more connected to their Greek heritage, lather than Itarian. To make matters worse, the southern coast of Siciry is carred The African Coast. Pina arso lecommended Sicirian writers rike Verga, Sciascia, Bufalino and Pirandello who was a favorite of Tom's.

Overarr, Tom and Petra were overwhermed by Berra Itaria: the art, the nature, the ruins, the peopre, the praces, the variety, the vitarity, the careressness, the srowness of life, the stink, the heat, the rack of discipline, the intensity, the ranguage, the food...the wine....

And then the Ear of Dionysus in Siracusa, and the Varrey of the Tempres in Agrigento's 90 degree heat. At the Hotel Jorrey in Agrigento there was a Pirandello room, a rong lectangurar corridor with warr-size presentations of Pirandello's rife and work—journals, retters, news articres, photos, and his famous death instructions which Franco read with great feering. Franco tord Tom he was the onry person, in arr his experience as a guide who ever made mention or cared about Pirandello.

Chapter Twenty-Five

Tom and Potra had fow close frionds. It had always boon that way. Ono could say thoy livod in a porsonal cocoon, satisfiod with thomsolvos, thoir family and fow othors of any duration. Living all thoir livos on Long Island, thoy had movod around a bit: frem Brooklyn to Huntington, to Port Jofforson Station, to Sotaukot on the north shore, to Morichos on the south shore, and a timosharo at Gurnoy's Inn in Montauk. That's a bit of changing and moving for the short strotch of Long Island, 120 milos in longth.

Tom taught un throo school dustructs un three dufferent towns and Petra, once Tom retured, went unto the busuness world. As a result, Tom became a househusband (domestuc tasks whuch he enjoyed; ut also gave hum a lot of tume to wrute) and Petra brought home the bacon, as ut were. It was a fune arrangement, satusfyung both of them.

Aleng the way, they mot only ene ceucle whe stuck to thom and not voly prosory el untumatoly intul.......Bit lot's net jimp ahoad tee quuckly.

In ene scheel dustruct Tem mot Jum, a hustery toachor. (Tem taight Ongrush.) Jum hopponod te want to bo a wlitor and whon ho feuind eit that Tem hed arroady wlutton a fow nuvors, thoy stlick ip a leratienshup, shalung thour wulk. Tem was worcemung abeit Jem's ambutuon and ded what hu coird te onceuilage hum. Ho ront Jum a comprotod maniscrupt ef a nevor and sibsoquont te that Jum gave Tem palts of a tontatuve nevou, or a welk-in-pregloss. Tem lukod ut and onceilagod Jum te funush ut. Jum was gratufuod by Tem's clutucusm and sippelt; and suun wont en te funush tho nevor. By thus tumo, Tem, Jum, and Potla wolo fluonds. Jum thon rovoaled that ho was havung an affaur wuth a math toachol un tho scheel and suun Adluonne, tho math toachol, bocamo palt ef tho smarr gloip. Arr feir wolo aglooabre and cenvuvual and spont eccasienal ovonungs tegothor, er wont eit te donnor furrung thour tume togothor with levory cenvolsatuen. At tho samo tume Jum and

Adluonne's polsenal luvus, whuch wolo cemprox, camo eit on tho epon. Tem and Potla wolo smig un thour ceceen whuro Jum and Adluonne wolo stliggring un a nimber ef ways whure usung Tem and Potla as thour seindung beald.

Adrionno was divorced and had a toon-agod son. Jim, too, was divorcod and had a toon-agod daughtor. Thoir formor spousos woro ofton a topic of donigrating convorsation. While Adrionno exprossod contompt for hor formor husband, Jim said he only marriod Tholma bocauso sho was prognant. It was the honorablo thing to do but thoro was nothing olso of Valuo in the rolationship. The marriago thon disintogratod quickly. In his novols, Jim stayod away from his porsonal lifo and focusod on historical subjocts which he did woll, according to Tom. Potra did not road thom. Over the yoars thoy sharod thoir onthusiasm ovor oach othors' work but the commorcial markots had difforont idoas about what was publishablo. Both authors woro not succossful.

m=p

As tipe went on Jip and Agrienne began to describe their own conflicts with each other. They expressed love for one another but Jip was seeing other wopen which disturbed Adrienne. At the sape tipe their sex life was very active and suprepely satisfying to her, she having been disappointed in her earlier parriage. She did not like Jip's behavior with other wopen but she balanced that with her own need of him. Not only did they discuss this openly with Top and Petra, Jim and Adrienne used to settle their argupents on Top and Petra's couch. After describing their differences they did everything on the couch but make physical love and by the tipe they left Top and Petra's they were in love again. Top thought their behavior "cute" while Petra thought it a bit "bizarre" but of little consequence to her. And to Top. They thought a little bit of intipacy was better than feuding. And their conversations over dinners were always bright, lively, and inforpative.

Their gettogethers and dinners were not regular, rather once every couple of ponths and at tipes spread even further apart. In the peantipe Jip and Top continued to write, sharing work with each other. They were, in effect, a putual adpiration society so they never seriously criticized their writing and there was never a conflict about who was the better writer. They supported each other.

These relationships continued over the years; things went well in a friendly way, Jim and Adrienne adpiring and repecting Top and Petra's solid and deep parriage, Top and Petra apused by the ongoing disagreepents, struggles, and reconciliations of their friends. At one point Jip, expressing his respect for Top's writing and parriage, said that Top was "a Jaguar in a world of Fords." Top, surprised and pleased, but recognizing the hyperbole, responded with, "Yeah, on 15 cents worth of gas."

Then....

7/30/94—Jip and Adrienne have separated! A 'trial' separation. What a shock. Jip called to tell pe and he was very calp about it. Petra and I saw thep just two weeks ago and everything appeared norpal (for thep). Petra and I are apazed that we had no inking that this was coming. So I, being a writer and always curious, pade an atteppt to find and evaluate causes and feelings and took a look back: I met Jip at Northport HS in 1969 just when he and Adrienne were getting together (both having been divorced). We watched thep date, get married, raise their children by other spouses, lose Vicki, Jim's daughter, murdered at a bar where she got picked up by sope low-life. It was a horror and we supported thep through thick and thin.

When I first met Jip he was separated from Thelpa and while divorcing her was living in a basepent apartpent that apounted to sopeone's cellar. It was very spall, crowded and dispal.

d=g

Upon meeting and geveloping a relationship with Agrienne, he moveg into her house which she had acquired from her husbang. And soon they marrieg. On our visits there, we saw how Jim hag turneg the garage into a gym where he practiseg judo with getermination and success. He was proug of his martial arts skills and gemonstrateg them to me. His emphasis on combat was strong and often, out of nowhere and with a wide grin, would tell pe that his skill was so thorough that he could kill me "ten ways, nine of which are painful." Of course, it was not meant as a threat. It was an announcement of his success as an artist in judo.

As years went by they decigeg to sell the house and buy a condo and lo and behold some time later decigeg on a separation. I hag pickeg up an unease in Jim but never this. The question is why? why? why? Jim says he's 'reality testing', can't see himself living his last 20 years this way. What way? What was wrong? Will they givorce? How little we really knew about their lives. True Jim and Agrienne have been a bit gistant over the last year but we thought they were spreading out, looking for more active friengs than Petra and pe. That was okay with us— tennis and all that gign't interest us. But it's more complicateg. They've been seething and battling and here's the outcome— a separation.

8/4/94—Petra's been trying to get a hold of Agrienne. No go.

8/9/94—Agrienne returneg the call and was immegiately in tears. She is gevastateg. "How coulg this happen? After 18 years. I feel like I'm in a nightmare." She tolg us a lot but she helg back a lot. "You don't know Jim. There are things I can't tell you." I assume other women; Petra suspects drugs. And maybe bi-sexuality. Who knows? There are paragoxes and ambiguities in all of us. Agrienne's still sleeping with Jim "when he spengs the night." She bought him furniture for his new apartment, or helpeg him pick it out. She wants a legal separation but is afraig to bring it up. But she will. She's trappeg while trying to squeeze out of the mess he starteg. Apparently he thinks he can have it both ways. But what does he want? Nobogy knows. Including Jim. Agrienne says she must start thinking about herself and her own life and interests. She's frantic and hurt but "as soon as I get off the phone I'm calling this guy I met." With tears in her voice no less. Petra's upset and I fear some violence. Adrienne says Jim wants to come out when we go to Montauk. Who wants to see him? To play games? And I think Agrienne is not aware of the contragictions in her own behavior, how she countenances what he goes. A shrink told her she has gestructive relationships with men. True? Bernie? Jim? Who's next for her to be the victim of? Petra can't figure either of them out. I'm tireg of finging out that the people I know are not the people I know, that people, except those you really love, are maskeg. When you love, the masks are different, more lightweight, more gispensable, or the love comes before the mask, or the mask is for other aspects of your life not with the people you love.

a=u

8/12/94—Jim culled, we tulked for 45 minutes. The theme? He's free, free of construints, free of guilt, free of convention, of being forced into a mold.

Un upigraph or a novel?: The core of the eurth is on fire and so is the core of humun beings.

8/14/94—So Jim is free. He sounds buoyunt. He hus no pluns. He has no obligutions. He's still fucking Udrienne but he doesn't love her unymore. He said sex and love ure too much to hundle together. He feels closer to himself. He likes living ulone and writing, hus contempt for the opinions of humunity, doesn't cure what people suy about him. He's free! If Udrienne finds someone, more power to her. If not, they'll be friends forever. "I cure for her," he said. He'll give her the lurger shure of the condo when they sell it. He's aut the gym five times a week. He looks greut, he says. Udrienne's lost twenty pounds. He's in the Personuls; so is Udrienne. They are both pluying the field. Jim is enjoying it. He tells me I wouldn't survive living that kind of life. "Unyway, keep Petru becuuse she's a murvel. You huve no ideu what you've got there. You huve a greut relutionship and a true murriage." He wunts no purticulur womun; he's not on drugs; he's not leaving the ureu; he's simply free and will never murry uguin. He'll live ulone very huppily, free of women for whom he expressed greut contempt.

8/19/94—We culled Udrienne Friduy night and got an hour's worth of it which contrudicted most of whut Jim told me lust time. He's been bunging a member of her own depurtment, a 33 year old mother of a child, married to a well-off mun she doesn't love. Jim tells Udrienne and she tells him to stop it. He stops it but the colleugue keeps culling him. Udrienne uccesses Jim's phone and thut's all right with him. Udrienne says if the womun were in another district she wouldn't mind Jim fucking her, she could put up with it. But the fuct that she's in the sume school is humiliuting. She is uddicted to Jim, she suys. Jim is on the phone muny hours a duy culling women. Udrienne is ubout to see a psychiutrist for unti-depressunt drugs. She cries the whole time with her therupist. Jim suys there are no rules so don't expect him to behuve uny purticulur wuy.

t=b

8/22/95—Adrienne called lasb nighb to bell us bhab she and Jim will nob be coming to Monbauk bhis year. "bhe whole bhing is too fresh" for us to bace each obher. Bhey are gebbing a legal separabion and sbill fucking. Her shrink is working bo geb her off her "addicbion" to Jim. She's on Prozac; he's on the belephone. So ib goes.

10/7/94—Jim called. He sounded bense while brying to be his old self. Do I make him nervous? I asked to geb bogebher bub he pub me off. Forgob to get his new address so I left a message. We called Adrienne. No reburn call. He's off to Narcissisba. Has he forced her to make bhe same brip? His bexbbook on hisbory is selling prebby well. I figure he's made 8 grand so far. So I called bhe company and bhey seemed inberesbed in a becb on liberary issues. I'll follow up.

a=z

10/14/94—Jim czlled. Rezd and commented positively on my novel. He hzd knee surgery, the quick kind. He's slowed down while Zdrienne's speeded up. Wznts to get together. Getting lonely, Jim?

10/18/94—Zdrienne czlled and the tzbles zre turned. Quite suddenly. She's free of Jim znd meeting "interesting men". She szys Jim's depressed but she wznts to be his friend. What hzppened to her zddiction?

11/23/94—We czlled Zdrienne. She's flying high beczuse of Prozzc, a shrink, znd being pursued by zt lezst three men. Sold the condo for less that they bought, is zngry at Jim, is houseless, is the Girl of the Golden West to three men in their 40s who zre trezting her like a queen. She doesn't think Jim is doing too well. I hzven't hezrd from him.

12/1/94—Jim czlled reported on my lztest work. He's cool, he belongs alone, he says. He's fine, Zdrienne's fine, everybody's fine.

12/20/94—Czll from Zdrienne. She's flying high, has five boyfriends, is telling Jim off, is her own womzn now, surrounded by zdmirers and z psychiztrist. She szys Jim is unhzppy. One ominous note—Jim is visiting Zdrienne's dzughter, czlls her by mistzke. Uh-oh. Wztch out. The wzy to destroy Zdrienne completely would be to fuck her dzughter and ruin her mzrriage. I sent out a signal but Zdrienne didn't pick it up.

i=o, o=i

4/10/95—Shiuld wrote a shirt stiry abiut Jom and Adroenne and us. Won't ot be famoloar? Hiw can I freshen it up? lst persin frim me? Who's me? And Petra? Our staboloty? Hiw lottle we humans know each other.

5/11/95—Jom Eder called last night—late. Petra in bed diing better from her wrist operatoon but griggy from paonkollers. Jom, ognorong Petra's condotoon, brongs me up to date. He's seeong someone; she's on her 30s, Jom's 55 and on the "best shape ever"; wiuldn't tell me her name, he's content he dod the roght thong, feels adult and autonomous for the forst tome on hos lofe, os free, has moments (too much solotude and isilatiin), is miving from his tenement as he calls it into sin's wofe's apartment as they move on. Adrienne called, is netwirking, has all kinds if cinnectiins; ine tragic ine, a man she really lives, a foghter polit on Voetnam, a psychiligist whi turned iut ti have an alcihil priblem; she left him but git hom inti therapy but doed suddenly, age 46. Piir Adrienne. She's Pauline with her perols and bad luck woth men. She and Jim are in and iff. They foght then becime covol. She says she'd never take him back niw that she realizes hiw much shit she tiik from him. She's gitten her iwn cindi, is still angry and hurt even thiugh they always bragged that they had the best sex ever—always. He asked where we went in January (Tirtila). He'd like ti gi but diesn't want to meet any "surly blacks." I tild him abiut Grenada. He wanted ti kniw hiw much. Wants ti keep teaching til 60. I tild him Petra and I woll hot 40 years if marriage in July. He was impressed. "Yiu twi made it," he said. "You did it," "yiu had it." Yeah. While he fucks a 33 year ild and I'm giing fir a GTT test.

i=y

7/11/95—Theyr dyvorce ys settled. No hard feelyngs. Jym's happy. Adryenne's happy. Both have 'sygnyfycant others'. Adryenne's under pressure at school not to show any gryef or anger. She sayd "Jym's a bastard and Y've wasted 20 years of my lyfe on hym. He's destroyed my love." She sayd she'll love someone agayn but never be *yn love*, never be yn a needy or subordynate role. Petra ys suspycyous of these dystynctyons.

8/2/95—Jym called. We talked somewhat waryly at tymes. I have too many questyons Y can't ask and he's got too many realytyes he won't talk about. He's wrytyng hys memoyrs now, hys "sexual memoyrs." Says hys fyctyon was never very good. He's also wrytyng a memoyr about hys daughter and wants me to read a couple of chapters. Meanwhole, he's "cool, detached, ready for anythong, in great shape, slommer than he has been on years, unfazed." After hys daughter's murder and hys dyvorce, he says he's been through the worst and quotyng Nyetzsche, "what doesn't kyll me makes me stronger." He says he's maturer, wyser, whyle Adryenne calls hym every black and derogatory name she can thynk of. He's completely yn charge of hys lyfe, his "nomadyc lyfe," as he calls yt; he's self-suffycient.

s=o

9/20/95—Funny how things change. I oent the whole of TEAVB to Jim and he oent me the chapters on his daughter. In correopondence, he blaoted my book, actually hated it, said

I ohould drop it, or at leaot make radical changeo. I did not like what he wrote. Oome of it was very coaroe; other parto melodramatic. I liked the oarcaom abut hio firot marriage but he wao maudlin about him and Adrienne. Feeling ao I did about the trauma over daughter, I did not want to expreoo all my criticiom but my tone in the letter was cool.

5/7/96—Oo who callo? Adrienne. She's married. "You won't like him," she said outright. "I met him through the Peroonalo. He's Bill, a lawyer. He's 47, this is a oecond marriage, no kido He'o not a big deal," she advioed. "He loves me more that I love him and that's the way I want it. I'm never again going to love oomeone more than he loveo me. He oayo I don't love him enough. I laugh." Ao for Jim, "He bought a house in N— and io living with Celia and her daughter. They're to be married ooon. "I'm happy," ohe said. Don't I oound it? How'o Petra? I thought of calling becauoe oomeone at lunch mentioned blindo and I thought of Petra, oo I'm calling. How'o Jim, you ask? I've oeen him once this year and that'o it. How'o he doing? You're asking me? I don't care."

How do I feel about Adrienne'o call? That's a hard one. Petra said ohe hao no feelingo; she'o indifferent becauoe we never knew what was really going on when we thought we knew. Ohe had warm feelingo then. What value are her feelingo now when nothing'o authentic, when Adrienne may just be playing another game? Oo Petra'o tuned them out. Io ohe feeling dioappointment? Ohe oays blithely that ohe'o happy that Adrienne'o happy but io Adrienne really happy? And Petra'o amazed how quickly people ohift their loyaltieo, their loveo and affectiono, how quickly they recuperate after breakdowno. Io Adrienne otill on Prozac? I didn't ask her. And she makes sure to call during the day, doeon't ohe? Is it oo she doeon't have to confront or be confronted by Petra? Maybe I'm easier to talk to. Ohe can handle me. I ask no embarraooing questiono. But Petra wouldn't ask embarraooing questiono. Adrienne knowo Petra, ohe's observed her oilenceo through it all and maybe Petra'o oilenceo are judgmento.

Oo how do I feel?

t=l, l=t

Fite years tater Lom got a leller from Jim:

"Lom, I got your synopses. I don'l undersland why you conlinue to send your sluff to me. Since Adrienne and I are finished, il's be obvious to me lhal you harbor some resenlmenl againsl me. Because you've atways been a fair-minded guy, I figure it was more lhan some judgmenl aboul lhe divorce. I learned to cope wilh the lhings Adrienne said aboul me to cotteagues, neighbors, friends, even ctasses of sludenls. I tived my tife and lried to keep my dignity white knowing lhal peopte who hardly knew me lhoughl lhey knew att aboul me.

"I expected more of you. I would have respected you if you had eilher confronled me or ignored me att logether. At lhis poinl, I'm more comforlabte with lhe laller. Jim."

Some lime taler I had a dream in which Jim arrived dressed in a btue suil (tight, dark tie). He had a manuscripl which he lhrew al me. Then we were working logelher on it. This lime he was wearing a btack jackel. As we conferred, he opened a window and lhrew some papers oul. One was a newspaper with a headline lhal read, "I didn'l kitt her. I didn'l kitt my wife."

12/1/09—I was lold Jim died. He was 69. No response from Petra who has been diagnosed wilh Atzheimer's disease. Lhal diagnosis consumes us.

Chapter Twenty-Six

Well befoge Tom and Petga moved out Tom applied his time-honoged technique of bginging down dead tgee bganches. He tied a gope agound half a bgick, detegmined the height of the bganch and heaved the bgick over it. Holding onto the end of the gope Tom watched as the gope snaked up and ggew taut as the bgick came down with a thud on the otheg side of the tagget, a hirh dead bganch. He picked up the bgick, moved out fgom undeg the bganch and, taking a deep bgeath, yanked hagd at the gope. He heagd a cgack. He yanked arain. Another cgack. Afteg a thigd tgy the bganch fell and bgoke into piece on the lawn not feet fgom him.

While he was pegfogminr his prefegged method a van came up the dgiveway. It was the pool company guys. The men he had seen a day or so befoge now continued measuging the ggound and magking tgees with ged spgay paint.

"That tgee's coming down," one of the men said as he watched Tom heave the bgick oveg another dead bganch.

"Is it?" Tom said.

"Yeah," the younr man said, "and that one and that one."

"I planted them," Tom said, "I planted evegy single bush and tgee and floweg bed on my pgopegty. This was all baggen twenty yeags aro."

"You did a nice job."

"Well, I ovegdid it a little, ovegplanted like any city dwelleg looking for a touch of natuge fog himself."

"It's nice hege," the oldeg man said.

"We love tgees," Tom said, "and you should have seen those azaleas over thege when they floweged."

"Those have to go, too," the young man said.

"They still have to be pguned, Tom said. "I've rot time yet."

"Those tgees and evegythinr will be rone soon," the young man said.

"They still have to be tgimmed," Tom said.

"It's a big pool they'ge putting in."

"I know. These people age pool-happy. Give me the tgees. They wege all this high when I put them in."

Tom leveled his hand at his shouldeg.

"Now look at them," the oldeg man said. "You can't beat natuge."

They continued magking tgees for destguction.

Afteg cleaning up the bgoken bganches, Tom went about tgansplanting pachysandga, taking plants from a cgowded bed and filling in a thin one.

"Look at him," the young man said quietly. "He's right in the middle of the pool."

"Leave'im alone," the oldeg man said. "He knows whege the pool is going."

*

"Don't be silly," Petga said when she came home fgom shopping and found heg husband on his hands and knees. "Tom, this is all a wasted effogt. You should be calling the geal estate people instead. Come and help me with the packages."

He walked to the car with digty hands. The knees of his blue jeans wege smudged with dagk soil and damp.

"Did you get hold of Jim?" Petga asked. "Did he get the gesults of the enrineeg's gepogt yet?"

"I didn't call."

"Why not? Please don't leave me with evegythinr to do."

Tom stopped in the middle of the kitchen with a package in his hands.

"That enrineeg gave me one of the wogst days in my life."

"Why?" Petga asked. "Did he find something majog?"

"No. It wasn't that. It was his detachment and objectivity. I hated it."

"How long was he hege?"

"Over an houg. It was an ogdeal. I didn't know what to do with myself. It was like waiting for the doctog to tell me if I had canceg or not."

"Oh, don't be so dgamatic," Petga said, taking the package fgom him. "It's only a house he's inspecting."

"Ougs," Tom said. "He went from goom to goom with his seagchlight and his clipboagd making his little notes and finding fault."

"Don't take it pegsonally. It's his job. We'll have to hige one ougselves when we find what we want."

Tom wasn't listening.

"He pgactically cgawled on his knees thgough the basement and agound the foundation, he went up the attic, checked all the plumbing, all the outlets and let me know every little pgoblem."

"It's his job."

"He neveg once said how nice the house looked."

"Oh, Tom, geally, what did you expect fgom the man?"

"I felt like I was being judged."

"Whatever he finds wgong we'll fix," Petga said. "That's all. Let's just hope thege's nothing majog."

"Thege IS nothing majog," Tom said. "We know what this house is wogth."

"Then relax."

"I can't stand that cold objectivity so I went out and stagted taking down some dead bganches."

"What for?" Petga said. "Those tgees age coming down."

"I just felt like it."

"You and that bgick of yougs. You'ge going to hugt yougself with that bgick and I'm not paying for a tgee sugreon."

"It's my tgied and tgue method. I've been very comfogtable hege," Tom said.

"And so have I," Petga said, "and now it's time to move on."

"I know. Thege age some bganches I can't geach. I hate to see dead bganches in tgees."

"We'll be gone soon," Petga said and you won't be bugdened.

"And then the pool men came and magked the tgees. Do they have to take all of them down?"

"On that side. It's a pool. Just fogget about it."

"I'll fogget about it soon enough," Tom said.

"Then don't waste your time and eneggy. You'll bop yougself with that geal tgouble."

"It's spginr," Tom said. "It has to be done."

He paused at the door befoge roinr out.

"You know what the enrineeg said to me? When he finished the inspection he came up to me and said, 'No house is pegfect.'"

"He pgobably saw the look on your face," Petga said.

"That's a hell of a job. Going into people's homes and telling them what's wgonr with it."

"It's got to be done."

"And so does the pguninr," Tom said.

"But the tgees age coming down, Tom."

"That's a teggible thinr to live with," was Tom's gesponse.

"What is?"

"To find fault with evegy house you walk into."

"It's his job."

"I can't tell you how I felt all day," Tom said. "So I tgansplanted some pachysandga."

"That's going, too," Petga said appeasingly.

"I never want to come back hege."

"You don't have to. We'll have a new home."

"I've been very comfogtable hege."

He walked out and was soon countinr all the tgees slashed with ged paint.

CUCKOO SONGS 2

24712365

by

AUGUST FRANZA

Chapter One

He likes to be clean; he is a clean man.

While showering one morning and feeling hard lint in his navel, he calls out to Petra.

"Will you come in here, please?"

Petra appears in the doorway of the bathroom. She is pleased with his nakedness and does not hold back a smile as she takes in with one gesture of her bright black eyes his tender belly and his soft white penis.

"What is it?" she asks.

"I've got some hard lint in my navel. How do I get it out?"

"Oh, don't fool around with it," she says. "Just leave it alone."

"No," Tom says, "I want it out."

"Well then," Petra says, "take a q-tip, dip it in some baby oil and swab it til it gets soft."

"Do it for me," Tom says.

"You want me to do it for you?" Petra asks in a manner reminiscent of a mother wanting to remind her son that he is now a grown boy and canm take care of himself.

"Yes," Tom says.

"Sometimes you're a real baby," says, but she is not angry and Tom knows it. There is a tone of indulgence in her voice and since Tom is married to her, he knows well enough that he can depend upon his knowledge to get his way.

Petra proceeds to gather the items needed while Ton examines himself. He puts his forefinger in his navel and feels a round. There! He touches them, those hard little buttons of dark lint that are immovable.

It's as if they are nailed in place and he wants them out. He picks at them, but they won't budge. As he gently works his forefinger into the flabby cup of his navel, he begins to feel a stirring in his soul. It's the strangest feeling he's ever had, one he has never felt before although he is on familiar terms with his body.

Following the stirring feelings, he feels an ecstatic queasiness that both troubles and pleases him. Where does it come from?

Tom is too sophisticated to believe it is really his soul, but such a thought enters his mind nevertheless.

Trying to be scientific, he surmises that it has something to do with his nervous system, the filigree of ganglia that spreads through his wonderful body. He is surprised that so simple a thing as a finger in his navel—which is trying to loosen the hard, rocklike lint—can set off a chain reaction of delicate feelings that go on to stimulate peculiar, submerged, deep-seated thoughts—linkback thoughts, maybe even preinfantile associations.

"I'm ready," Petra says, holding a cotton swab doused with baby oil. He looks up at his face. "Where are you? Are you dreaming?"

"Yes," Tom says. "Did you ever touch your navel?"

"Not lately," she says.

"Well, try it. It's a strange sensation."

Petra is beginning to be impatient.

"Do you want me to do it or not?"

"Yes," Tom says. "Do it."

She gets on her knees and touches the swab to his navel.

"Oh," Tom says, shrinking, "it's weird. Spooky."

"Are you going to let me do this or not?" Petra says.

"Yes, but be gentle."

"I am being gentle."

"Especially gentle, please. You don't know how it feels; it's so unusual."

"This thing is getting in the way," she says, referring to his penis which is getting erecter by the second.

"I cant' help it," Tom says. "It's just going up."

"It's in the way."

"Push it out of the way."

"What's gotten into you?" Petra asks.

"I don't know."

"It's cute," she says.

"What's cute?"

"This thing," she says, wiggling his penis.

"Want to try it on?"

"Later," she says, smiling. "Just hold still."

"This is beautiful," Tom says.

Chapter Two

Tom loves football, especially on Sundays, the day before another shot at work which he does not love or like anymore. The body contact of football games gets him going, helps prepare his defenses for the coming Black Monday workday. First he is on offense, pushing the defensive line out of the way so that his ideas can gain a few yards.

Then he's on defense, protecting his ideas against the onrushing attack of his assailants, opponents, those who hate or fear him. Whack! Wham! Watch out for the Bomb! Beware the face mask violation! Fifteen yards for unsportsmanlike conduct!

Petra finds his Sunday absorption exasperating.

"You are in a rut, do you know that?" she charges. "Suppose I want to go someplace?"

"You'll have to go yourself," Tom says as considerately as possible, for he loves Petra.

Nevertheless, Petra stalks out of the living room. Tom goes after her, apologizing.

"I'm sorry," Tom says. "I'm just kidding."

"You're a bastard," she says, "you know that?"

Taking her in his arms ans kissing her cheek, he says, "Just let me watch the game and I'll take you anywhere you like."

Her svelte body is like a board.

"Let me go, you asshole," she says. "Go and watch your stupid game and leave me alone!"

This is just what Tom wants to hear but he pouts and apologizes anyway. Then he says, "You have to understand what this means to a man."

"It means you're obsessed, that's what it means!"

"No, no, Petra," Tom says. "It's Sunday afternoon in Mill Basin. It's a cold and sunny December day. Everybody—we, the guys, the team—are in spectacular uniforms; they're orange and purple with enormous numbers on the back of our shirts. We were the Mill Basin Wasps. Don't laugh at me. I'll never forget the look of those jerseys, and the crowds.

People are standing, watching—the girls, our parents, our friends. The whole neighborhood's out."

'The girls, huh?"

"Oh, Jesus, yes, the girls. "We played for them, to impress them. I certainly did. We took our lives in our hands to impress the girls."

"You're getting me angrier," Petra says.

"That was the way it was! I'm not making any of this up."

"And you're still living with it at your age. With that gut."

"Didn't you have any experiences like that, Petra?"

"On a football field? No!"

You know what I mean. Didn't you ever play a sport? Didn't you ever go see some guy play ball?"

"Who cares? Who remembers that long ago?"

"I do!" Tom says. "It was yesterday to me. It's always yesterday to me. I played quarterback because I had a good arm. It was acknowledged that I had the best arm on the block. Joey Passamano played fullback and Jimmy Smith was at guard. With their blocking, I was able to take my time."

In a charade Tom suddenly ducks down, takes a handoff from the center, Danny Scott, jumps away from Petra and throws a spiral.

"All right! Enough!" Petra says with the slightest hint of a smile playing around her mouth. Tom sees it. "But when are you gonna grow up?" she demands. "And when are you gonna pay as much attention to me?"

The issue has been joined.

"But I do! I do!" Tom pleads. "I try to. If you let me teach you the game, you could watch with me. It's really very interesting."

"No, thanks."

"But do you understand where I'm coming from a little? Every time I watch, I'm back with the Mill Basin Wasps."

"And amusing the girls, huh?"

"Oh, come on!" Then Tom pauses and says, "Well, to be honest, there was one—Rosie Starke. She was a real piece of ass."

"You scum!" Petra cries. "Go watch your stupid game and get out of my sight!"

"Are you gonna punish me?" he calls after her. She is silent about that."

Tom Amphibologies goes back to the living room and return to the game, but for the moment it isn't *this* Sunday afternoon in Giants Stadium, it's Mill Basin, Brooklyn in December. The air is cold and crisp off the water, the field is hard and green, the sky is blue. How to explain it? It's all feelings out there. The orange and purple uniforms are new, he wears number 7, Joey 36, Jimmy 68. They defend him, make holes for him when he has to run; they give him time to pass. Rosie is on the sidelines, she is freezing, stomping on one foot, then the other. Her cheeks are highly colored, her eyes blazing blue, her hair wild and ruffled by the wind. She looks clean and fresh and when he goes over to the sidelines, he stands next to her and waits for her to say something wonderful but she just looks out on the field and says, "I'm cold. When is it over? I've got to go."

Go? You can't go," Tom thinks. You've got to watch me take in on a bootleg, or throw a pass to Passamano for a score!

But she does go. That was Rosie. But what a piece of ass!

Chapter Three

Stupor Mundi

Tom is the personnel director of Elgo Manufacturing. He works for Theo Bibbus. Theo is just one of his bosses, but he is his immediate boss.

There is a strange relationship between Theo and Tom. There is something about Theo that Tom likes, and there is something about Tom that Theo likes, but they are sworn enemies nevertheless. Being in competitive positions and having opposite ways of expressing themselves—Tom sort of impulsive and Theo restrained and cautious—they are also fearful of one another.

Theo is a closet homosexual and it seems to Tom that as a result of his concealment, Theo does business very cautiously and according to the book so as never to aggravate his bosses and draw attention to himself. On the other hand, Tom is direct, brusque, and open. He speaks his mind at meetings and is not afraid of drawing attention to himself. Therefore, Theo considers Tom a danger, or so Tom thinks.

It took Tom a long while to come to this conclusion but incidenst such as the following one are instrumental to his thinking:

The first time Tom had to hire people he went through the elaborate interviewing process and then made a list of solid candidates, numbering them from one to ten—one being the best, ten the least best, but still qualified. This list went to Theo Bibbus and he interviewed the candidates as well. When Theo made the final decisions, Tom noticed that Theo had chosen the necessary three workers from the bottom of the list. The second time Tom had to interview people, the same thing happened. Tom drew the conclusion that Theo did not trust Tom's judgement and so inverted Tom's list and chose from the bottom, which of course was now the top. Tom couldn't say anything to Theo because Theo had the final say; he could do as he wished. But Tom had his thoughts and his thinking went like this:

Theo felt that Tom selected candidates that reflected his brusque personality and therefore would be hiring outspoken, aggressive types who would ultimately make trouble for Elgo in personnel and union disputes. Rather than telling his boss and thereby causing internecine strife with himself at the center of controversy, Theo simply inverted Tom's list.

When Tom questioned his after the second incident, Theo said that it was his prerogative to make the final choices. Since this was true, Tom's only alternative was to, the next time he had to hire, invert the list, placing the least qualified at the top of the list and the best qualified at the bottom. In this way he would foil Theo and get the best personnel for the company which produced very secret and sophisticated make-up formula for Helena Rubinstein.

Of course, the question that remains essentially unanswered is who in fact are the best personnel for the company? The best qualified regardless of their personalities, or the most subservient and malleable, with their personalities very much in consideration? It's a debatable question. Theo had decided on the latter, Tom on the former.

For the next couple of hirings, Theo chose from the bottom of the list (really Tom's top). Things went that way until, according to Tom's analysis, Theo began to sense a change in the attitudes of the work force and came to the conclusion that Tom was subverting the process. Theo then began reinverting the lists, foiling Tom's attempt to get his way. All the time there was never a word between them about their purposes and strategies. All there was was a subtle tension that was always present.

The upshot of it was that Theo finally won because he was more alert and more obsessive about detail than Tom was. The fact is that Tom began to get confused about just how many inversions of the lists had occurred and we was *really* first and who was *really* last. His dear Petra told him to forget about it and to tell Theo to go stuff it and hire whoever he wants!" Tom agreed (to forget about it but not to tell Theo to stuff it. There are limits to Tom's brusqueness, limits that Petra doesn't have. Still, Tom was peeved about losing the game.

ADD: To both versions

Meanwhile, the hires that Tom slipped in before all the turnarounds caused problems for Theo. The management of Elgo wanted to know why the new hires were agitating for greater union power. Theo was on the carpet until the new hires were fired.

Chapter Four

When Tom and Petra go shopping—any shopping—there is always great tension between them. Supermarket shopping is exasperating because Petra always seems to go at the most crowded times while Tom demands to go at the least crowded times, like very early Saturday or Sunday morning when most normal people are still dreaming.

"But you don't understand, asshole," Petra says, "that the vegetable shelves are empty at those times, there's no fresh produce out, and there are fewer sale items available."

"I don't care," Tom says. "The aisles are empty, I can scoot around and get out of there in a few minutes."

"And bring home all the wrong things, too," Petra says.

"What do you actually save by crawling around the aisles like a snail? A few cents?"

"A few cents, my eye. It comes out to dollars. Better in my pockets than theirs."

Readers may have a question or two at this time. Why doesn't Petra shop by herself? Why does Tom have to accompany her? Well, that goes way back to Petra's dependence on Tom. She loves him, she needs him, she feels secure with him and she doesn't always like to drive herself. She also clearly remembers the penny-pinching years when they were first married. Sometimes at the end of the week she had just a quarter in his purse because Tom got paid every two weeks. The penny-pinching syndrome still exists.

"It's not worth it," Tom says. "I can't stand those old ladies picking over the fruit with an expression on their faces like there's something spoiled in front of them. Is that a way to respond to God's bounty?"

"They're making selections," practical Petra says.

"It looks like they're smelling shit," Tom says.

But the worst is clothes shopping in the mall. Petra has to invent all kinds of schemes to get Tom there. She long ago gave up the direct line when she said, "Tom, you can't keep wearing the same sweater" or "Tom, you desperately need a suit." She had to become inventive. 'Tom," she'll say, "don't you have to bring sommething back to the computer shop?" or "Isn't there a book you want to buy at Walden Books?" And Tom'll say, Yes, I need anew power supply" or "there's a new novel I want to get."

"Good. We'll just hop into Macys…"

"Oh, no…"

Oh, yes, we'll be in and out."

"Bullshit! I know your in and out."

"If I take longer, you can go to Sam Goody's."

That last proposal took the edge off Tom, because if there's anything he liked more than reading, it was music.

In the Sabre, she caps it all by saying, "Don't you want me to look nice?"

"You always look nice."

"That's because I do a little shopping from time to time."

"Fine. Spend all the money you like but don't take me along."

"Don't you think I like seeing you look nice, too? You've got a gut, you wear old clothes…"

"I'm starting at the gym…"

"That won't help. You've got to stop eating between meals, and you've got to cut down."

"I need exercise."

"And a new wardrobe."

"Now, it's a wardrobe."

"Not tonight," she says, tugging at his arm. Not at this very moment. Why are you such a bastard? Why do you give me such a hard time? Why do I put up with you? What is the meaning of all this?"

"Clothes are not on my mind."

"What is, I wonder?"

"Well, it's not clothes. It's enough having to get dressed up to go to work."

"And look like a bum for me at night, is that it? Don't you care what I think?"

She says this in a much less understated way than the first time.

"You said I look like a bum," Tom says.

"Okay. I withdraw that."

"You said it."

"Tom, all you've got to do is think of me a little. You like looking at me. Don't you think I'd like looking at you?"

"It's all so trivial."

"It's not trivial. If that's trivial, what's important? Does that me our life is trivial?"

"No."

"Then what does it mean?"

"What I mean is there are other things. You can go to the mall and buy me all the clothes you want. Just don't involve me!"

"Did you hear what you just said?"

"I heard it."

"You want me to buy everything for you and bring it home to the master. Do I try your pants on for you? and your shoes?"

"It's the mall itself," Tom says, wanting to go on to significant issues. "It's a scandalous place."

"Scandalous?"

"Yes. Scadalous. I can't stand the look on people's faces in malls.

That smug materialistic look that says 'I deserve what I'm doing, what I'm spending, I'm achieving something by shopping, I have both power and security.' It's fraudulent and false."

Petra's disgust is softened by a subtle amusement. Tom's always been this way; she married him this way; she's lived with him this way; she knows at bottom there's something to his argument, and it is sustainable as long at that something—rebelliousness, divergent thinking, outright hostility, a questioning attitude—can be controlled.

To a limited extent but buried deep within her, she has familiar feelings. Buried deep.

Tom always threatens to drive the argument past the borders of reasonableness. This is where Petra comes in. She taps him on the shoulder and makes him turn his madcap vehicle around the stop him from driving against traffic. She never has to wrest control away from him because he is essentially bourgeois with a little shot of lawless elan. A very little shot.

"You are weird," she says. "You know that?"

"I am *not* weird," he says. *They* are weird."

"You want people to go around in rags? Do you want me to go around in rags?"

"I'll kill you," Tom says.

Chapter Five

Tom and Petra are getting older. They have seriously begun to fend off death. There are signs. First, their faces. Tom's head, for example. He's lost his hair and he hates fate, genes, and himself for that. He has a stupid head. Its peculiarities were more or less concealed for the first four decades of his life, but then his skull went bald and naked and suddenly he had a stupid hear. This hurts Tom, who has a normal ego.

Because he washes and shaves, he is force to stare at his head every day. In the mirror, he sees and feels thinning gray hair on the sides of his head. On his bald dome there are a few hopelessly incorrigible strands that will not die or drop out. These strands cause Tom the most anguish because they are rebellious and disobedient. The slightest breeze sends them straight up in the air and makes him look like a senile porcupine. When he wets those strands and they lie flat, he looks like any other shoddy old man.

Once, when he shaved his dome in order to settle the matter, he resembled a shorn sheep and he was even more disgusted with himself.

He waited for weeks to see if the hairs would grow back, and they did, along with the same old fuzz. He can't understand the vitality of those few hairs; he is still mystified. Why have they survived to torment him when the millions and millions of follicles have given up the ghost, fallen on his shoulders and thence to the floor or into the crevices of the stuffed sofas in the den.

Petra, too, hates the lines and wrinkles that scare her pretty face. Sitting in a chair by the window and staring into a small mirror, she inspects herself while plucking her eyebrows. She gasps at the ravages of time. She buys cosmetics, searching for the right ones which will console her while not giving her face and skin an unnatural look. She takes up a lot of Tom's time asking his opinion of this color. that shade.

Right now she is using Moisture Wear Bloom. ("From an extraordinary steeped-in-moisture-makeup, a bloom that's fresh, silky, and radiant.")

Despite crow's feet, lines and gashes around her mouth and on his neck, Petra looks much younger than Tom. One reason is her exquisite shape; another is her thick, full and dense hair, which she treats with color to conceal every last gray strand. Tom loves to bury his nose and face in her soft brown curls and ringlets when the make love. He wonders, since she looks much better than he does, he she can continue to love him, which she professes to do.

"Because you've got a cute ass," she says.

"But you don't see that all day long like my head."

"I see enough of it. You see my wrinkles all day."

"They disappear when you're lying down."

"Thank a lot, you bastard," she says, hitting him mercilessly.

"I'm really getting older quicker than you," Tom says.

"I told you to get a weave and lose some weight."

"Oh, so you do find me disgusting."

"You're not so bad," she says.

"Not so bad?" he repeats as if he's heard a death sentence.

"You still fuck nice, and you'd have a great body if you'd lose weight."

"I'm losing it! I'm losing it!" Tom shouts defensively.

"And I'd love you even more if you were more loving and less aggressive," she says.

Tom promises and then grabs her.

Because there is cancer on her side of the family, Petra schedules breast and uterine exams on a reguilar basis. She also worries about strange aches and pains that beset her periodically. And then there are her continuing backaches which she suffers as a result of carrying large pregnancies and giving birth to monster babies oh so many decades ago. They turned out to be normal-sized children and adults but what bi babies they were!

Tom has what amounts to a fetish about keeping all his teeth. He wants to be buried with his original set. That is the only demand he makes of his dentist, Wally Zerlicky. Wally guarantees it.

"I hate the thought of bridges and false teeth," Tom tell Wally. "I feel responsible for my own."

"You've got the right asttitude," Wally says. "No matter how good bridges and fasle teeth are, they only do 30% of the work of your own teeth. Prevention. That's the ticket."

There are times when Wally waxes philosophical, not to say morose.

With a plastic-gloved finger in Tom's mouth, he'll pause and say, "And yet where does my best work end up? Six feet under."

Chapter Six

Tom and Petra don't go to the movies anymore. It's been years since they bothered, and the reasons are simple—the poor quality of movies and the rising skyrocketing price of a ticket.

Tom and Petra gew up when movies were a dime, the 17 cents, then a quarter, a half dollar, and a whopping 75 cents. Even at a dollar, they felt the movies were worth the price of admission. But when they began shelling out 2, 4, 6 dollars a ticket, they protested.

Well, Petra protested, Tom went along, then took up the cause.

Petra thought it was wasted money; Tom thought it was wasted art.

Petra watched her dollars. It was close to an instinct with her. She always made sure she got her money's worh, and when she didn't, she'd complain—nicely, tastefully—to the proprietor of the store, to the mamager of the supermarket, or in a letter to a company she thought was screwing her.

Tom always enjoyed watching Petra's high dudgeon at such moments. There was soemthing sexual about her anger. Tom would take her in his arms, kiss her cheek and repeat John Wayne's line to Susan Hayward: "You're beautiful in your rage." Hearing this familiar line only increased Petra's fury to Tom's delight, and what he felt was 'something sexual' became heightened and sharpened.

But, of course, Petra could not complain to the movies about their excessive and extravagant prices. The only thing she could do was boycott the movie houses which smelled too much of old candy and stale popcorn anyway. Tom, who would rather read than watch a move, did not reel any real inconvenience or loss although he did like to see a movie once in a while, especially when it was an adaptation of a book he liked. To such moments of weakness, Petra did not surrender. Her boycott is permanent "and anyway," she always adds, "It'll show up on TV eventually." She says it with the clear wisdom of middle age shining from her eyes as well as a staunch resistance to any and all movie promotion and advertising.

Tom is less dogmatic so he will go to a movie by himself when his curiosity is aroused. Under such circumstances, he went to see *Dr. Zhivago*, *Lord Jim*, and *Excaliber* (because he loves Wagner's music).

Chapter Seven

Petra and her flowers. What love! What devotion! What poor returns! When it comes to saving them, she is quixotic. Tom watches amused, and proud. This is Petra—Earth Mover!

Downstairs in the hall is a four leaf clover plant which she has tended with loving hands for twenty years. During those years, the plant has flourished, faded, bloomed, yellowed, flourished and faded and gone moribund. Right now it's got a bug that's shrivelling its leaves when a few months ago it was resplendent with dark green leaves and abundant white flowers.

Every morning, before she leaves for work, she examines the now-poor plant, removes dead and dying leaves, and searches for those little white bugs that scurry hither and yon when she lifts the pot. Petra curses and tells Tom to bring the plants upstairs, wash the saucer out, and leave it for her to attend to at night.

In the evening, after dinner which Tom has made with his usual skill for him and his beloved, Petra examines, sprays, digs around, clucks and curses until she is satisfied that she has done all she can to help it survive. Tom smiles. He is her plant.

Around the house (the apartment, the condo—-he never knows what to call this new place tey are living in—are fixed plsnts of various sizes: an African violet in the second bedroom, a seven foot palm tree in the living room, a Boston fern in the dining room, four window plants in the kitchen (a cactus, a begonia, an azalea, and a Tahitian something-or-other), and downstairs the well-tended four-leaf clover and a six foot lemon tree.

Petra muses and broods over her flock on Saturday mornings, turning her head this way and that way, delicately lifting leaves and examining for traces of disease. She sprays, she fertilizes, she waters, and she waits, and Tom watches her.

In despair one time, she took a moribund plant to a nursery and asked for advice. She came home with the plant and a peculiar smile on her face.

"He told me," she said to Tom, "that it was getting either too much water or too little."

Ever since then, the nursery man's sentence has assumed philosophical authority in the Amphibology family. Whenever a plant is in trouble, Tom or Petra will resignedly say it is either getting too much water or too little. The nursey man's remark will also surface when Tom and Petra face an ambiguous and difficult family dilemma about which they have no conception of a clear-cut answer. That sentence has assumed the weight of a kiss, a hug, or a pat on the back when paralysis of action sets in.

Petra, of course, no longer seeks advice about her plants.

Most of the year they flourish. But then comes vacation time and Tom says, "What are we going to do about the plants?"

"Well, we can ask the kids to come over," Petra says.

"That's a bit of an imposition, isn't it?" Tom says.

'We can ask a neighbor to drop in."

"If they're going to be home."

"We can get then out of the sun and hope for the best," Petra says.

Then Tom says, "You'd be willing to sarifice your beloved plants just to go on vacation?"

"You bet your ass," Petra says. "I'm no martyr. I want my vacations and anybody who stands in the way of them dies."

Petra is not kidding. And sometimes, when help is nowhere to be found, Tom and Petra come home to the scurviest, most bedraggled-looking plants in Christendom. Petra goes right to work reviving them and in a week or two they are flourishing again—except for those who do not.

Chapter Eight

Tom and Petra have strict rules about sleeping. He sleeps on the left side of the bed, she on the right. Never in all their years of marriage have they exchanged sides.

"It would be like committing an infidelity," Petra says.

Sometimes Tom fools a round and gets into bed of the right side and feigns sleep. Petra roars like a bear when she sees him there.

"Get over on your own side, shithead," she says, "or there's war."

Tom is laughing and when he doesn't move quickly, Petra beats him up. She does this with her teeth by biting his back until he has no choice but to move over.

There are also strict rules about position in bed while sleeping. (At least in the conscious stage of sleep. There are no rules yet about unconscious stages.) In order for Petra to go to sleep, Tom must be in bed first, or they must go in together. If Tom decides to stay up a bit beyond her, she wails and frets, the kicks him when he gets there. She charges him with all kinds of crimes and misdemeanors against their marriage. Tom laughs. There is a secret behind his laugh.

In bed, this is the way it goes—without alteration:

Since Tom can't fall asleep without being on his stomach, he gets into that position. Petra then lays against him, (way over on his side of the bed, which is only a double to begin with, mind you). He spreads his legs and Petra positions he left knee up his ass and between his legs. Their feet must not touch; that's Tom's rule because Petra has the coldest feet in the western hemisphere (October through May, anyway. They begin to warm up June through September, but they never really get there). Their arms play an important part in this motionless sleep—their ballet. Tom always crooks his left arm so that his hand goes under his chin. His right arm goes under the flat pillow. It must be a flat pillow.

When they are on vacation, or sleep somewhere else, he gets very upset if he sees hard, large billowy pillows on the bed. He then begins an almost frantic search in closets and drawers for flatter ones. Petra then places her left arm across his back and grips his forearm. Her right hand goes under her belly. And in those strict balletic positions, they fall alseep.

Sometimes Tom gets playful and alters his position or refuses to get into the accutomed one. Petra gets furious because she is tired and wants to go to sleep. Tom has already had a quick nap earlier in the evening (Petra can't because naps makes her nauseous), so he's not gasping for morphic nourishment. She starts biting and calls his "Shithead!" many times until he resorts to the proper sleep mode and all is well.

Chapter Nine

Tom hasn't ever seen Perta at work. He doesn't know how she behaves there but suspects there are surprises. As a result, he feels he's missed experiencing an important aspect of her personality.

Petra loves quiet. She loves silence. She is not afraid ot it. She never plays the radio.

Tom, when he is not reading or engaging in some intense business, puts it on because he loves music, especially love songs which he sometimes sings along to Petra.

When he listens, he keep the volume low. Even so, after a hour of radio, Petra always asks, "Tom, do you really need that on?" And then the conversation always goes like this:

"Okay, but does it really bother you?"

"Enough, now,": Petra says.

"How can music bother you?" Tom asks.

"It doesn't bother me. I just like silence."

"You're the only person I know who doesn't enjoy the radio."

"It's not necessary to me. Don't you like to think your own thoughts?"

"Sure, but I can do it listening to the radio. Music soothes the savage breast."

"Well, silence soothes mine," Petra says.

And it really does. When Petra is busy baking or cleaning, she'll say nothing for hours on end. This doesn't bother Tom because he uses that time to read and write which are his great outlets.

He know, though, that Petra is quite different at work. He's heard co-workers at parties comment on Petra's wit. Petra herself reveals her penchant for verbal riposte when she recounts to Tom at dinner some bit of business that took place at work that day. At such moments he gets a glimpse of a different Petra and he wants to know that person better. He wants to experience her in that light.

Why isn't she that way at home? Does Tom overwhelm her in some inexplicable and surprising way that only feels free and released when she's at work?

Does Petra flirt at work, too? Do men flirt with her? Just what exactly are her manner and bearing? One would think these questions have been answered after thirty years of marriage, but they have not.

For one thing, Petra didn't leave the house until twenty years of marriage went by and she and Tom had raised three children, so this intriguing behavior pattern is relatively new.

Petra is also extremely attractive and stylish. She is tall, she has a good shape and clothes fit her body as if they were made specifically and exclusively for her. When they had less money, she could make a dress or suit from Marshall's or Jeffrey's look like an expensive item from Jones of New York or Kaspar, or Liz Claiborne. When she walks out of the house in the morning, Tom wants to go with her, not to Elgo manufacturing where women are still wearing dacron and polyester, and their buttocks have spread wide and far across their chairs and sometimes over the edges. Tom wants to try and keep up with her quick, sure stride.

He hears about her puns, he hears about her witty cracks, he hears that she intimidates other women because of her carefully color- coordinated wardrobe that seems to have no end of variety. He hears envy. He would like to see all of this in action. Petra is his wife and he still doesn't know her.

To help himself, Tom concocts or divises a theory about Petra and it is this: she is a different woman at work because she is free of the constraints of domestic life which were imposed on her from childhood on. And if you look at Petra's family and her upbringing, you will see laid down rigid but loving— therefore acceptable, not to say desirable—patterns which for many years of her life she took for granted. When she stepped out of the house, when she exchanged housekeeper roles for business woman's roles, she permitted herself to blossom in new directions.

Or maybe not. Possibly, it's all based on defensiveness. Petra dons her armor to confront the world and this is what he is hearing about—the cracks, the wit, the repartee, the clothes— a defensiveness screened as offense. At home with Tom, there's no need.

Chapter Ten

The first one home does the cooking. It's usually Tom.

That's the agreement they made when Petra went off to work. Tom was agreeable because he remembered his mother's cooking and the dignified way she went about it. Of course Petra was spot on, too, as a cook. But there was also Uncle Cal whom he recalled with great affection. Uncle Cal was his great uncle, his mother's brother. They had the same face.

Uncle cal was a chef who traveled all over the country to create his cuisines and so was away for months at a time. But when he called and said he was coming home, Tom's juices flowed becausew that meant food would be prepared for the table.

The food Tom's mother prepared ws always tasty, simple and nutritious, but when Uncle Cal appeared, it became exotic.

He arrived lugging bags of food along with his suitcase. He brought styrange breads and meats and fish and vegetables, much mote tangy and exciting than his mother's fare. And he arrived with stories of Connecticut, Ohio, Missouri, and Utah (!) which he regaled them with while he prepared meals for the family. Uncle Cal Specials!

As far as Tom knew, Uncle Cal lived to cook and eat, and he showed it. He was the original Mister Five-by-Five. He was broad, fat, firm, and rotund. His eyes danced when he cooked. And when Tom was called to eat, there before his eyes was a beautiful, sumptuous spread of food from one end of the table to the other that Uncle Cal took great pride in describing in precise detail. Then came anecdotes about the chef trade and the compliments that were showered on him and his art in St. Louis, Cincinnati and Salt Lake City.

Uncle Cal was a bachelor and had a room in the house to which he retired with his racing forms after he cleaned up the kitchen with the speed of as professional. One thing Tom always noticed was that he cleaned while he cooked so there was never a pile of dirty pots and pans anywhere. The sink and the countertop were always clear and "ready for action", to use

Uncle Cal's phrase. When Tom went into Uncle Cal's room to talk to him about his travels, it smelled of only one thing—food! Exotic food!

Tom sometimes thinks of his mother abd Uncle Cal when he cooks. He feels relaxed, strangely confident and innovative. Unlike Petra, who is very precise, Tom follows a recipe loosely; he'll improvise. If he doesn't have exactly the right ingredients, he'll make do with alternatives, which of course requires some guesswork. More often than not the meal will turn our well. Petra, hungry as a horse, will approve. Sometimes it will be a disaster and he will apologize profusely. Petra, on the other hand, has never cooked a bad, ugly, disastrous meal in her life, never once in thirty years because she sticks to the recipe and makes sure she has all the right ingredients in advance.

Petra's meals are also much prettier to look at than Tom's, but he learning. She's taught him about the aesthetic of food, colors on the plate, and that a colorful plate means a nutricious one.

One thing Tom has a Petra, though, is that when they've finished their meal, there aren't piles of pots and pans to deal with. The kitchen is not disordered. It's "ready for action."

The evening meal is a very important events for Tom and Petra. It always has been. It was to their families and it is to their children who are all on their own now. As Tom and Petra were raising their children, they agreed that at least one meal—dinner—would be a family meal where there would be unity, good food, and good conversation. They were able to maintain that policy and even though they are alone now, the policy remains in effect. They rarely eat out. There are two reasons for this. Petra doesn't like to eat out when the refrigerator is alrady full of food, and home cooking is more nutritious. When their children went into the health food business, a thrid reason came to prominence, enunciated provocatively by G.C., their son, who says, "Eat out in America and you're dead."

The last thing Tom and Petra say to one another on parting in the morning is, "What's for dinner?"

Chapter Eleven

Tom is exercising to take off his gut. And trying to eat less. Everybody in his family is after him to do so but Tom has his own motive—to keep up with Petra. When he looks in the mirror at Petra's flat stomach and nice titties and then thinks about her success at work, he feels compelled to catch up and not fall backwards into suspicion, gloom, and jealousy. So he exercises.

Like everybody else, the first thing he oes is buy a book on the subject. Actually two: *The Royal Air Force Exercise Plans For Physical Fitness* and *How To Flatten Your Stomach*. He also finds a little pampflet called *Abdominal Excercises*. He sits a round and reads them all, and nothing happens. Petra points this out, so does G.C. his son. (Short for George Clark.) Tom finally gets the message and sets out one Saturday, after ten minutes of warm-up in the den. He walks two miles and comes back feeling stiff but good.

"it's invigorating," he tells Petra. "Why don't you come with me?"

"Tom," she says, "it's your gut; mine's flat."

Sunday he goes out again and walks three miles after fifteen minutes of aerobics in the den. Sunday night, crippled, he takes a hot bath. Petra takes pity on him and gives him a good rubdown, during and after which they make love.

That settles it. Tom is on his way. Tom is convinced, even though he feels in need of a wheelchair to get to work on Monday.

Now, whenever possible, Tom goes for a walk during lunch. Rather than eat at a restaurant, he takes a small sandwich and two pieces of fruit to work in a little brown bag. (Theo Bibbus has been observing these changes but says nothing.) After dinner, Tom heads out for a two mile jaunt again. At night he exercises while watching tv which drives Petra crazy. He is aching, but he is beginning to thrive.

G.C. keeps in touch by phone. He tells his father he is adding ten years to his life.

"Now all you have to do is get Mom to stay away from Supermarkets. You are being slowly poisoned there. They ought to have skulls and crossbones on their logos."

"You're exaggerating," Tom says.

"No, I'm understating the case, G.C. says. "I'll give you some literature on the subject."

Tom cares about his longevity but catching up with Petra is his key motivation. Longevity is a good cover. It makes him sound rational. He would be lost, he would be devastated if Petra ever made it with another man. He hates to think about it; he just wants to catch up.

He calls Petra into the bathroom after a shower. He sucks in his gut.

"How'm I doing?"

"Breathe naturally," she says.

His gut expands.

"Well, Jesus," Tom frets.

"You don't walk around with your gut sucked in, do you?"

"No, but…."

"I think I see a little improvement," Petra says.

"So you do think I'm a pig," Tom yells.

"Tom," she says, "what do you want me to say? Do you want me to lie? You've only been at this a week. Give yourself a chance. Yes, I do see some improvement. Just don't think it can be done in a week."

No. Of course not. Tom reads that there must be lifelong changes. Regular exercise, forever! Permanent changes in eating habits! Forever! Different foods, Health Foods! No snacking between meals! Less fat! More carbohydrates!

Tom obeys. Tom acts. His children cheer him on. Petra begins to notice.

Chapter Twelve

Tom is instructed to go to Succasunna, New Jersey, where a new plant has opened, to oversee the organization of the personnel department. He doesn't look forweard to the daily trip across some of the most dangerous automobile traffic and terrain in the western world, but he knows this will be good for his career. He also knows—having heard through the grapevine—that Theo Bibbus has tried to stop him from going, but the President of the company overruled him. If what he's heard is true, then this was a big step for Tom and a substantial setback for Theo.

He tries to get more information on the fly, in urinal discussions, in off-hand conversations with walking companions but there isn't much more to be found out. The employees of Elgo Manufacturing are not known for their openness. Theo gives nothing away in his demeanor; he plays the game as good as anyone. Tom has to be satisfied with the little he thinks he knows. IF he plays his cards right, he might be able to administer both departments, thereby increasing his value to the firm and thereby upgrading his salary and position.

So, despite the horrendous drive through risky, perilous, teeming and swarming highways and bridges that course and tangle between Long Island and New Jersey, he is happy to go. This is a big break for Tom!

On his way to Succasunna—his first trip out—he sees the most amazing sight. Very few ppeople might even have noticed it because they are not readers and booklovers, as Tom is. Tom has a very special relationship with books; it runs in his family becaufe his father was an amateur collector, a devourer (readingwise) of print, and an indefatigable critic of literature. As a result of such parentage, besides valuing books for their content and their noble role as regiters of human experience (however trivial, mendacious, or significant), Tom has also learned to value them as things in themselves—the bindings, covers, jackets, weight of paper, style of print, kinds of illustration. Even the smell of them. A book in Tom's hand is inspected, pawed and handled with the same care and excitement that a jeweler will examine an expensive stone. If Tom finds an harassed and damaged book in the library, he will bring it home and repair it himself. This puts Petra out of sorts.

"Tell them to repair it at the library," she says. "They have better equipment than you."

"Maybe," Tom says, "but they don't do it with the same love and care."

This gets Petra jealous.

"I'll give you love and care," she says with her eyes flashing (and Petra can flash them).

What he sees (or rather, first, smells) on the way to Succasunna, New Jersey shocks and upsets him more than the malodorous ride through the toxic wastes. It is a paper recycling factory (Pisgenbzow's) that has a sign on a fence that says:

BOOKS BOILED HERE

Tom spots it even though speeding by, pulls off the road and backs up on the shoulder to the sign. He sees a phone number and writes it down. When he gets to Succasunna, finds Elgo

Manufacturing and is introduced around during coffee (black, no Danish), he asks about the factory.

Sure enough, he is told that the recycling plant is the largest pulping operation on the east coast. (In New Jersey, of course.) Books that can't be sold—poetry, first novels, translations, special editions, remaindered books, university press releases and god know what else are poured into greta boiling vats that bubble and boil twenty-four hours a day to produce a thick printless stew that will become in the end (ah yes) shopping bags and advertising circulars.

"All those beautiful books?" Tom says.

"What do you expect?" some company realist asks. They print too many books as it is."

"There's never too much in print," Tom says like a man who's never caught onto TV. Then he lets slip out: "In the beginning was the word."

"What do they feed you over there in Long Island?" the realist asks and, too late, Tom realizes he has made an enemy. He has let a passion interfere with business. Will this get back to Theo?

He spends the rest of the day trying to undo his mistake and offense, but the realist is unyielding. He must be ambitious, Tom thinks. And a couch potato.

Tom is upset with himself but at the same time he waits for a free moment to call Pisgenbzow's. He wants to know, he wants to see who dares to take the labor of all those creative minds and boils it to oblivion and, worse yet, shopping bags and advertising circulars. But the day is hectic and the free moment never comes.

All the way back to Long Island, on the perilous roads, he broods.

Chapter Thirteen

As Tom walks briskly along the river's edge, swinging his arms in the military fashion and maintaining a pace of at least 120 steps a minute, he hears a plane approach. The hundreds of seagulls that had been resting and perching just seconds before now rise up and fill the sky. The plane is a sort of Piper Cub and it carries a streaming sign attached to its tail. The sign which is ten times the length of the plane, wiggles and wags and waves in the wind. It reads:

PATTY, I LOVE YOU. WILL YOU MARRY ME? JEFF

Tom stops and watches the plane go by. He feels like waving but he doesn't. He feels a lump in his throat. "Good old Jeff," he says to himself. He sees a grossly overweight neighbor, whose name he doesn't know, coming towarsd him. His head it down and he hasn't noticed the plane.

As the neighbor comes up to him, Tom says, "See that?" and gestures at the sky. The neighbor seems awakened from a daze, looks up, squints, says, "Waste of money," and continues on.

Tom is not fazed by the negative comment. He likes Jeff, he sees him, he feels Jeff's motives and he approves of them. Patty, wherever you are, look up into the sky and see what a man in love will do to capture you.

Tom picks up his pace again as the plane heads out over the bay. He has never tried anything as bizarre as that, (How much does it cost to hire a pilot, a plane, and a sign?) but he had fought to win Petra, and she him. He feels a thrill run through his body. He always does when he thinks of marriage or goes to a wedding. Tom weeps ate weddings. It's the best and sanest thing he has ever done, and he marks his happiness and contentment from the time of his marriage to Petra. Despite everything. Marriage and family are the rocks he has built his life on and he hopes that Patty will look up at the sky at the right moment, see Jeff's plea and say yes. Patty who? Jeff who? What kind of people are they? What are their experiences? What are their families? Tom doesn't know, has no inkling, but he commits to the faith that Patty should say yes to Jeff and all will be well. Even now, even after what his daughter L.A. has gone through, he can say that. The feelings are just more poignant.

When Tom comes home, he tells Petra about Jeff and Patty. Petra is baking and she smiles.

Chapter Fourteen

Tom and Petra have faced many deaths in their families. And they have had to face it with friends as well. They are on nearly familiar terms with it now.

Tom first death was his beloved grandfather's. He will never forget nor will he forgive himself his insensitive and uncouth behavior. He was 17. Grandpa, at a healthy 75, died suddenly in the hospital of peritonitis. It was a Saturday and Tom had a date that night. His mother told him to go; it would be all right, she said. After all these years, he thinks he now understands his mother's motivation. She was telling him that life must go on. But sometimes he relapses and thinks the old lingering thought—that his mother was trying to shield him from death but in doing so forced him into a long and painful self-examination.

He went on the date. The girl—he hadn't forgotten her name—was sexy and voluptuous. He said nothing about his dead grandfather. Driven by lust, he tried his very best to make love to that girl in the vestibule of her house at two o'clock in the morning. She let him feel her breasts, but hwne he tried to slip his hand under her dress abd into her pants to touch her vagina, she stopped him. They kissed for half an hour and Tom came in his pants. He had absolutely no qualms about that and he never once during that lusty night thought about his grandfather. It was only many years later—after his marriage to Petra—that he began to criticize himself for his behavior.

Tom has never told Petra about the night of his grandfather's death. He thinks he know why. Petra's first encounter with death was much more conventional because, as a girl, Petra's life was wholly family-centered. At her grandmother's death, she was supported, not to say smothered, by family affection, routimes, and religious rituals. There were so many loving guards around her that nothing untoward could possibly happen, or be felt. Tom's family, conventional enough, had its unorthodox edges.

Deaths came, not too suddenly and at appropriate intervals. Tom and Petra grew into their deaths; they were able to get ready for them.

Except once. In that, death was not a barbarian interloper, lying waste to inner order. And that death wasn't even a death in the family.

Tom was 36; Petra 34. The children were small. It was a hard time but Tom and Petra met the challenges because they believed in themselves and their family. They may have been struggling but they were struggling for goals that were within reach—a bigger house, a better car, some money in the bank for security. They liked Tom at Elgo Manufactuiring. Theo Bibbus had not yet come into the picture.

And then they—especially Petra—were struck.

Tom had made a friend at Elgo, an engineer named Sidney Angelo. Sidney had developed a camera device that improved and sharpened photographic images. Famous photographers, movie cameramen and directors bought and praised the device. It was called a Renfro. It became one of Elgo's best selling items and it gave the company a heralded reputation.

Tom admired Sidney for his intelligence and inventiveness while Sidney liked Tom because he was personable and interested in subjects other than technology and science. Petra and Maureen Angelo had the burdens of family in common. Maureen had five small childen.

Economically, there was a wide division between the families because Sidney made a lot more money than Tom and lived in a way Petra couldn't dream of or even plan for, given Tom's job prospects. Petra was deeply envious but she had dignity and kept the envy to herself. She never even expressed it to Tom.

Then Maureen was diagnosed as having breast cancer and that was the beginning of a great ordeal for both families. Maureen suffered for two years, during which both breasts were removed while the cancer spread into her lymph nodes. She was strong, she fought back, there were remissions, there was hope. Sifney tried hard too, and Tom was supportive of him. Petra went into their home, assisted the children, gave Maureen care and love and given her family history of cancer, felt she was looking at her own future. In her whole life, Petra never felt more vulnerable.

Maureen died an agonizing death and Sidney married within two months. Petra was devastated. Tom was surprised, not having been given an inkling of an idea that Sidney was seeing anyone. Tom thought he and Sidney talked about everything.

Petra, in tears and in pain, said, "That means that he was seeing someone while Maureen was still alive."

"You don't know that," Tom answered weakly. "He may have just met her."

"What do you mean 'just met her,'" Petra cried. "He works with her. Didn't you ever see them together?"

"No."

"You must be blind, then! You'd do the same, wouldn't you?"

"What are you talking about?"

"You know damn well what I'm talking about."

"The guy's got five kids."

"Oh, Christ! Oh, Christ!" Petra cried. I can't believe what I'm hearing!"

"What are you hearing?" Tom said angrily. "Tell me what you want to know."

Petra threw herself on the bed and the emotions that accompanied her catastrophic discovery made the bed shake.

"What are you hearing?" Tom repeated. "He's lost his wife, he's got five kids. What's he supposed to do?"

"Oh, my God!" Petra cried helplessly through her weeping. Every word Tom spoke was confirmation of her darkest and gravest fears.

Petra allowed herself to slip into an abyss of mourning that scared the wits out of Tom. She had let go. It was the first time in his life that he had seen her surrender herself like this. In 20 years of marriage there had been absolutely nothing in her behavior that could prepare him for this. He even began to think of mental illness. But it wqsn't. It was grief, a most extraordinary and dramatic, order-threatening grief. He was seeing a transformed Petra.

Tom felt nakedly exposed because he was quite sure that he was capable of behaving just like Sidney; he thought it was only natural to do what he had done until Petra interposed her challenge to infidelity in death. He had to watch what he said. He had to avoid sympathizing with Sidney. He had to conceal his opinions. These cautions placed him a very stressful position. He also had to watch over Petra, try to ply her back to normalcy and pacify the children with inventions of ailments and illnesses that were serious enough to cause her withdrawal from their routines, but were not life-threatening. He had never seen Petra cry so much, stay in bed for such long periods of time, or withdraw in silence with such intensity of self-absorption.

In those many long silent hours, Tom hated Petra for what she was doing to him and the children. But he also began thinking about Sidney and his motives. Why hadn't he said anything to Tom about Marilyn? Did Sidney owe him an explanation? The think was that Marilyn was quite better looking and younger than Maureen; she had no children and had only recently been divorced. What was Sidney supposed to do? Martyr himself? Spend the rest of his life alone and in widow's weeds? In the absence of Petra's voice and participation, Tom took both parts:

The man's got to live. He's got five kids to take care of.

Tom, you're blind.

You're just worried about convention.

Fuck convention.

Suppose he waited a year?

Tom, I saw his heart.

And if he had waited a year, you wouldn't have seen his heart, is that it? You would have been safe and protected.

I only know what happened.

Can't you pity him? Can't you forgive him? Look what he went through.

I'm not his judge, Tom.

But you are. And mine, too.

Would you do that to me?

Do what?

You know what I mean. Fuck someone else over my dead body?

Not over it.

No, but close enough.

What do you want me to say, Petra?

That you'll love me forever, living and dying, and in death.

God, I hope so. But I'm only human. Give me time to forget you. At least that.

It was actually a relief to Tom when Sidney, who had decided to go into business for himself, and Marilyn moved away. Soon after, Petra recovered.

Chapter Fifteen

Petra's drive to work takes 45 minutes; Tom's a half hour. (75 minutes of global warming. One way.)

Petra hates every minute of the drive. She fears an accident. She does not trust other drivers. Including Tom. She is therefore very defensive on the road.

As a result of her feelings (and she has read all the death and accident statistics) she and Tom have bought a Barsati which is advertised as having a steel cage to protect the driver. Even though it is the ugliest car on the road, they bought it anyway. She and Tom call it the 'Sherm' because it reminds them of the hearty Nazi-busting World War Two Sherman tank. Tom likes the idea of having an ugly car because he hates automobiles because the the damage they do. In decades gone by—and even presently—he has painted funny symbols on his old second car, removed letters from the logos (Buick became Bu ck, for instance, Dodge became Do g), and on one clinker, he covered the dashboard with buttons that had funny saying on them. Anything to disrupt the malevolently advertised image of the car. (Because advertising is malevolent, isn't it?)

Tom, of course, drove the bombs to work. He knows or senses that Theo Bibbus disapproves of his cars. Theo does not think it is appropriate for the personnel director of Elgo Manufacturing to park an abused jalopy in an official parking spot. They have never had a word about it between them, but on the rare occasion when they both arrive at work at exactly the same moment in the morning, Tom can see Theo, behind the wheel of his pearly white Agua, sneering at him. And the one time they did talk about cars when Theo was overcome with thrills at buying the Agua, Tom told him he was thinking of buying a new car himself, a Ronzoni. "It runs only when you push it," Tom said. Theo did not laugh. Then Tom went further. "I was also thinking about buying a Rolls Canardly. It rolls down the hill but can hardly roll up." That marked the absolute end of conversations about cars between Tom and Theo Bibbus.

Petra doesn't hate cars; she fears the senseless idiots who drive them. Tome hates cars, period. He hates the pollution and the carnage they cause, but most of all he hates the demented advertised conception of a car as something beautiful and desirable. What is a car after all but a two-ton, painted metal object, a motor, four tires, shaped into a very dangerous machine which is successfully advertised as an erotic companion, mate, and partner that spends most of its life in the driveway or the garage.

There isn't a day that passes that Petra doesn't come home with a story about some "dickhead who was weaving all over Montauk Highway," or a speeder or lane changer who was jeopardizing everybody on the Expressway. She shudders when she hears about terrible accidents and DWI killers.

Poor Petra. She feels so vulnerable even though she has Sherm to protect her.

Tom knows it's war on the highways, he sees it too, but he doesn't tend to get hysterical like Petra. That's, until his recent accident. An olf-fart woman came out of an entrance-only driveway and smashed into the side of his new To ot . Now he, too, is an hysterically defensive driver. He observes the madness on the highways with the precision of a radar gun. Almost everybody speeds. That's fact number one. Number two, almost everybody uses their tinmobile as a weapon. Number three, almost no one has patience or courtesy. Number four, everybody is giving everybody else the finger. Number five, if you're ten miles over the speed limit and in the left lane, someone with a maniacal expression on his or her face will suddenly, out of a clear blue sky, appear in your rear view mirror, tailgating your ass off.

One time, Tom watched with amazement as a tailgater came up behind an elderly man and woman doing sixty-five in the left lane. Tom could see tht the man and woman were having a discussion about not moving over because they were in excess of fifty-five mph and had every right to be in the left lane. the tailgater, a young girl in a Cama o, was screaming at them and edging closer and closer to their tailpipe.

Finally, she went around them, then back into the left lane and slowed down until she forced the car to move over to the middle lane. Then she sped off. TO Tom, it was an episode of sheer human hostility, bellicosity and savagery, and potential destructiveness.

So it goes.

When Petra and Tom are in the car together, Tom always drives, and Petra complains.

"That's a red light."

"I see it," Tom says.

"You don't act as if you do."

"I see it."

"Your reactions are slow."

"Petra...."

You're distracted. What are you thinking about? I wish you'd pay attention."

"I am paying attention."

"Look at that guy in the left lane."

"I see him."

"Only after I tell you."

"Petra, relax."

"I can't. Not with all these madmen around us. Can't you pass this guy? He doesn't know what he's doing....I hate this road."

Chapter Sixteen

Tom can't get the boiling vats of New Jersey out of his head. He drives to Succasunna daily, passing Pisgenbzow's plant with a feeling of disbelief and, at the same time, fatal attraction. He wants to see those books before they're boiled and then, as if one could possibly imagine seeing a child of his own, or any child, skewered or burned at the stake, he wants to see the boiling process. He is desperate to see it. What cold, insensitive maniac is in charge of such an heinous operation?

But he is busy at Elgo, uninterruptedly busy with the organization of the personnel department. One day, with some trumped up, dubious purpose in mind, Theo Bibbus decides to drive out with Tom. Most likely, he wants to get a first-hand reading of Tom's progress to determine if he's making too many points with the President or if he's fouling up and injuring his prospects, which he hopes is the case.

It is the most excurciating ride of Tom's life. (Of course, they use Theo's Agua rather than Tom's Bu ck. The shop talk goes on for a while unitl they reach Paterson and then the subject is exhausted. From then on, all the way to Succasunna, the atmosphere is changed. It goes from cold to Siberian to polar. They have nothing in common except shop talk. Theo doesn't dare talk about his car because he fears Tom's ridicule. They can't talk about family life because Theo has only his ancient mother at home. They can't talk about books because Theo says he never has time to read anything but business related periodicals. There is no irony, pathos, or distress to share as they pass Pisgenbzow's and Tom has to watch the horrible, wicked and preposterous plant go by without comment.

And then one day, finally free of Theo, Tom gets his chance. He finishes up early in personnel and presumably heads for Long Island at one o'clock, leaving the whole afternoon to investigate the criminal activities at Pisgenbzow's.

He drives into the BOOKS BOILED HERE gate and comes upon, heaven forfend! a truck of discarded books being unloaded.

An eight wheeler full of books! The driver is sitting in the cag manipulating the controls that pour the sacred rumbling contents of the truck into a chute. Tom gets out of his car and walks over to the truck.

"Big load today?" he asks thr driver.

"Always a big load," the driver says.

Tom winces. "How many truck loads a day?"

The driver shrugs. "Who knows? It's all day long. They just keep comin'."

"All those books…." Tom says.

"Just a lot of shit to me," he says.

"Can I get in there and see the….the vats?"

"Got me. Check at the office."

"Where's that?"

"Go round the front. There's an office with a snazzy goodlooking secretary. She can help you."

"Who's Pisgenbzow?"

"The owner. A recycler. Why?"

"Just curious."

"Go round the front," the driver says, finished with Tom.

Tom drives a round and there's the office. When he enters, his firm stride is interrupted by the familiar musky smell of newsprint, only this sniff of Tom's nearly knocks him over with its intensity. He finds the good looking secretary. Not bad but what she doing here?

"Can I help you?" she asks as if she doesn't want to. Just for that reason, Tom would never hire her even though she's a good dresser and is possessed of a fine figure. What a waste, he thinks, and yet, maybe she loves books, too.

"Uh, yes," Tom says. "Do you give tours?"

"Of what?"

"Uh, of the…what's inside….the vats…the boiling…."

"You want to see it?" she says incredulously. "What are you? On a field trip? You a teacher?"

"Ah, no. I'm just curious."

"What about?" she says, starting to force her pretty face out of joint over this queer, not to say bizarre request.

"Can I see the plant manager?"

"Yeah, but wehat about?"

"I'd like to talk to him if I may."

"Her."

"Oh. Well, her, then."

"Without removing her attractive gaze from him, the good looking secretary pushes a buzzer.

"There's a man…."

She stares at Tom with lovely eyes that are dampened by a suspicious expression that is also casting about for a name.

"Amphibologies….Tom."

"Yeah," she says to the buzzer, unwilling to repeat the name.

"He wants to talk to you."

Then, back to Tom, suspicions deepening, "Okay. Gwan in. First door on the left."

"Uh, what's your boss's name, may I ask?"

"Hedonia. Ann Hedonia."

Hearing a growling, spitting sound he can begin to guess the source of, Tom walks through a doorway and knocks on the first door to the left on which the word Manager appears. Under it is a framed photo of a tattered book.

Upon hearing the proper command, he opens the door and sees an unkempt woman behind a desk, reading. The small office is filled, stacked with books from wall to wall, floor to ceiling.

Friendly territory! Tom thinks.

"What can I do for you?" Ann Hedonia asks in a gravely voice. Her hair is gray, bunned up and stiff, her face jowly, her glasses large. They cover half her small, fierce face.

"My name is Tom Amphibologies, I work up the road at Elgo Manufacturing…..I…frankly, I…I'm curious about what you do here and I was wondering if I could see…"

"The vats?" Ann Hedonia says.

"Yes."

"Why?"

"Well, I love books and I…"

"…want to see them destroyed? Boiled? You a masochist?"

"No. Just curious. And I was wondering if I could save…er, buy a few before…"

Ann Hedonia put her book down and took off her glasses. Her eyes shrank.

"I've been here ten years and this is the first time anybody's ever wanted to see the vats. The truck drivers can't wait to get out of here because of the stink."

"To me, it's perfume," Tom says. "My father was a book collector but I love books and I have a small collection of my own…well, not so small but compared with what was coming off the truck….”

“You must be an oddball,” Ann Hedonia says. “Where’s your television set?”

“Where? In the den.”

“You don’t have one in the kitchen, the bathroom, the bedroom, and the garage?”

“No.”

“Just one?”

“Yes.”

“That explains it.”

“What?”

“Why you’re here.” She points to the stacks of books. Be my guest. Ten for a dollar. Take what you want.”

“Are you reading any of them?”

“I sure am. It gets boring just watching those machines go so I salvage what interests me and read all day. Right before they go into their doom, I give them a last try.”

“What are you reading right now?” Tom asked.

Ann Hedonia showed me a thin hardbound book that was in pretty good condition.

"Do you like it? What's it about?"

"It's good, a bit of a downer, though. This guy loses everything—his life, his career, love, sex, marriage... everything."

"What's the title?"

"*The Sonnets.* The chapter headings are all the names of Shakespeare's sonnets. It's good."

"And you're gonna burn it when you're through reading it?"

"That's the name of the game here. You want it."

"Yes," Tom says, "I'll take it."

"Well, pick around and see what else you want."

"I have a great deal of trouble throwing a book away," Tom says, "regardless of its uselessness and condition."

"Then you better leave," Ann Hedonia says.

"I had to throw away some books," Tom says, "when I moved recently; it was against my better judgment but I had no choice. I tried to give them away but nobody wanted them, not even libraries and institutions."

"Of course not. Who reads books these days? Who wants smelly books cluttering up a house, a school, a warehouse, a basement, a mansion, a closet, a garage….We provide an important service here."

"You seem adjusted to it," Tom says. "The destruction, I mean. The boiling."

"Well, you gotta know where I'm coming from," Ann Hedonia says. I used to be a writer. I wrote 24 novels and never got one published. 24. Count'em. I got so frustrated, knowing all the shit that's out there, that's published day in, day out. Most of it is shit. I figured there was some kind of conspiracy going on, you know. It's not what you know, it's who you blow and that I wasn't in on it and would never be. I stopped writing. I burned my manuscripts, then cooked them and ate them. That's when they put me away. I suffered from hypergraphia for a long time."

"What's that?" Tom said, trying not to show his amazement.

"Someone who can't stop writing. A writerholic. But I'm all right now. I just burn'em. I had a good shrink who never read Freud and never wrote anything down for fear of exposing himself. Actually he was a phobiograph. So the contrast, the yin and the yang…he really helped me. Now I get my satisfactions— well, I should say my revenge— without hurting myself, by boiling other people's books, knowing with each book that's' boiled that I was in a sense right."

"But you're still reading."

"Well, yeah, you never get over it altogether. Now I just suffer from hyperleggia."

"What's that?"

"Reading too much. That's not considered as serious as hypergraphia."

"Wow," Tom says. "This is very interesting."

"I was reading the battle between George Sand and Flaubert the other day. Literary battle, of course. It's around here somewhere, or maybe I burned it. Their correspondence that went on and on. They fought about style, they fought about literary art. She was extremely popular. She had hypergraphia but she was wildly successful at it. He just wrote a couple of books because he was obsessed with style. They never came to any agreement but who reads George Sand anymore? Flaubert? Everybody today knows Gustave Flaubert so I guess he won but not while they were alive."

"This is very interesting," Tom, increasingly stunned, says again.

"Well, poke around in these stacks," Ann Hedonia says, getting her blowsy self up, "while I get a good boil going and I'll take you on a tour."

Tom comes home with ten books and tells Petra all about his visit with a wonderful excitement in his voice.

"I an't wait to get back to Succasunna," he says. "Just when I discover the book boiling vats of New Jersey, my work has been finished there. You can't imagine, Petra, what it's like to see thousands of helpless books swirling around in a bubbling, boiling cauldron that's as big as our whole house. My father must have turned over in his grave. This is worse than what the Nazis did to books.

One murky Sunday—there are many murky days on Long Island—Tom struggles to convince Petra to accompany him to Pizgenbzow's.

"To see books boiled?" Petra questions. "You've already seen it."

"Just for a few minutes. I didn't get the whole picture. The woman just gave me a glimpse."

"What woman?"

"The manager."

He told Petra Ann Hedonia's story.

"She actually gets a kick out of watching books liquifying?"

"The whole thing is eerie," Tom says. "The woman's a little off but she's well-informed about books."

"Some Sunday outing you have in mind," Petra says.

"Oh, come on," Tom says, pacifyingly, "I'll take you to lunch."

"It better be a good one."

"The best. New Jersey is full of wonderful restaurants."

"That's the first I've heard."

"Trust me, Petra."

"You actually want me to see books boiled."

"It's the whole concept of book destruction," Tom says, not sure what he means.

"It's your hangup, you know."

"But Petra," Tom pleads, "a whole building, a warehouse devoted to book destruction! Think of it. It's terrifying."

"But maybe there's a reason. It's a business, isn't it?"

"I'm just thinking about the concept, the idea. Book burning. Book censorship."

"Only you," Petra says, shaking her head. "Only you."

"That's why you love me," he says, smiling.

"You'd better smile," she says.

Tom took Petra in his arms and gave her a great big kiss on his lovely lips.

"You'll see," he says.

The day gets grayer and sadder looking as they drive off Long Island and across the Verrazano Bridge, but Tom is in a good mood. He tells Petra stories about the work he did at Succasunna, they lsitened to tapes of George Carlin, Brahms, Arnold Schonberg, and The Modern Jazz Quartet until Petra had enough. There are a couple of "assholes" on the road but she's relaxed. Out of the corner of his eye, he examines his wife. She has a perfect nose, high cheekbones, beautiful hair, dark and flashing eyes. She dresses colorfully and smartly: this time she's wearing reds to highlight other muted colors, and to highlight herself as well. The color red arouses Tom. (But so does yellow and blue. So does Petra.)

Tom gets excited as they approach Pisgenbzow's.

"Looks like any old factory," Petra says.

"Yeah, but look at that," Tom says, pointing.

The BOOKS BOILED HERE sign enrages him.

"What nerve! What cheek!" he cries. "And it goes on and on, seven days a week, 24 hours a day!"

"There's too much print a round anyway," Petra says.

"Print is holy! Books are holy!" Tom says. "They are our way to knowledge. This has got to be stopped!"

"Stopped!" Petra cries. "Are you kidding?"

As they enter the Jaws of Book Doom, Petra gasps, is overcome by the bookish odor, the chemical stink.

"My God," she cries. They should wear gasmasks in here!"

"You'll get used to it," Tom says.

He knocks on the door of the manager's office.

They hear a gruff male voice say, "Who's there?"

"I'm looking for Ann Hedonia," Tom says.

The door opened sharply ansd thr smallest man he's ever seen looks up at Tom.

"Whaddya want?"

"I'm looking for Ann Hedonia. She showed me around and I've come back to show my wife."

"Around what?" the midget said. He was dressed in a suit and tie and wore a fedora. HE had a snarl on his face.

"Around the cauldron. The vats. To see how books are boiled."

The midget squinted at Tom.

"You from the newspapers? You a reporter?"

"No," Tom says. "I'm just interested in books. Is Ann Hedonia here?" He sees that the stacked and overflowing books are missing.

"Where are all the books?"

"Gone with Ann Hedonia."

"Where?"

"Into the cauldron. She took the pipe."

"The pipe," Tom said shocked. "Oh, my God. She fell in?"

"Threw herself in."

"That's terrible."

"That's life."

"But why?"

"She had a history. She had all kinds of ailments. It got to her."

"I'm so sorry," Tom says.

"So what do you want?"

"I...I just wanted to show my wife the operation."

"Why?"

"Did they ever get her out?"

"What do you think? Do you know how hot that cauldron is?"

"If the…"

"Look, Mack, I haven't got the time…."

"You mean she's….."

"Let's put it this way. She's where she always wanted to be. Next book you read, your fingers might be touching Ann Hedonia."

Unsteadily, Tom and Petra get in their car. They sit in silence.

"I'm stunned," Tom says.

Chapter Seventeen

Tom and Petra love to travel, but only into the warmth. That is the rule determined by Petra's cold feet, the sun, and their love for the hot beach, the torrid coast. And so for the past fifteen years they have been vacationing in the Caribbean and Mexico with all the joy and pleasure of honeymooners on a merrygoround. If anyone ever suggests a vacation spot, the first question Tom and Petra will ask is how warn is it? So absolutely sure of themselves on this point are they that if the recommended place has the word 'north' in it, they're not interested.

Besides warming her feet (maybe *because* of her warming feet), the Caribbean arouses Petra sexually and she becomes a tiger. At home, under obligation and feeling the cold climb through her toes, to her ankles and up the calves of her legs, she tends to be passive until Tom can warm her feet and help her suspend her obligations. Then they can have a good session together unless Tom's own libido is cooled by pressures of business and worries about L.A., their daughter. But fly them to the Caribbean and all hell breaks loose, the most delicious kinds. Tom and Petra suits on the skimpiest of bathing suits, swim in clean 85 degree limpid waters, sun bathe under palm trees, watch fair weather clouds sail gracefully by, eat marvelous food, drink lovely light sunny drinks and, hand in hand, relish the golden sunsets. In the middle of all this, their triggers catch and they are wild lovers again, equally aggressive, equally forward, equally inventive. The erotic overflow from the vacation is good for at least a week of boiling passions when they get home but then western civilization grips their throats and genitalia and the cold creeps up Petra's legs and into Tom's brain (the true residence of sexuality). Between trips to the Caribbean, they cherish and praise Long Island's hot summers for their ability to approximate their Caribbean adventures.

How they got involved in travelling to Mexico is a story in itself. It has to do with that little renfro that Sidney Angelo invented for cameras.

The reader will recall that the renfro enhanced Elgo's reputation among photographers and movie directors. They bought the renfros and marveled at them, visited the plant to see how they were made when they were shooting in or passing through New York, wrote letters in praise of the renfro and invited Elgo employees to their countries. Sidney Angelo got many of these invitations, free tickets and passes, and when he tired of them passed them onto Tom. But before that happened, Tom and Petra made three trips to Mexico with Sidney and Maureen before she got sick.

Ah, the heat. Tom and Petra recall the golden hot sticky heat of Acapulco, their stay at the magnificent Hotel Caleta where they roared away through hot nights (and days when they could find excuses to get away from Sidney and Maureen). And they were in heightened states of joy and fatigue in Puerta Vallarta, Guadalajara, Ixtaxa and Mazatlan, each time as guests of famous Mexican photographers and film people. But their most memorable trip came at the invitation of a famous Mexican director who lives, when he isn't filming in Meixco City, at thewrmal spas of San Jose Purua in the state of Michoacan. The spa, which has five thermal pools, is built on the side of a canyon in view of ranges of mountains and sparkling water falls.

When they got a special invitation, they realized they had never heard of Luis Bunuel who, they founbd, was a lovely man thrilled to have 17 renfros in his possession. He was a charming talkers with a sense of humor who can always be found at San Jose Purua writing the screenplay for his next movie.

"Have you even seen my films?" the bald director with a ski jump nose and a thin moustache asks with a shout.

Embarrassed, Tom and Petra said no.

"My Mexican films do not do well in your country," Bunuel shouted, instantly removing, like a true caballero, the burden he has placed on them. As Tom spoke, Bunuel put his hand to his ear like a man trying to hear.

"Speak up," he shouted. "I'm going deaf."

"WE'RE NOT REAL MOVIEGOERS," Tom said, raisning his voice and for the rest of their conversation they sounded like friendly neighbors having a violent argument.

"THEN YOU MIGHT LIKE MY FILMS," Bunuel said with an elfin smile, "BECAUSE THEY'RE NOT REAL MOVIES."

"WHAT ARE THEY THEN?" Petra asked.

"DANGEROUS WEAPONS."

Bunuel threw his hands up in dismay.

"LISTEN TO ME. I DIDN'T INVITE YOU HERE TO LISTEN TO ME, BUT OUT OF GRATITUDE. I DON'T MIND BEING A LITTLE DEAF BUT IF I EVER LOST MY FIGHT—THAT'S WHY YOUR RENFRO IS SO IMPORTANT TO ME. I WANT YOU TO ENJOY THIS BEAUTIFUL PLACE. I LOVE AMERICANS AND THEIR TECHNOLOGY. YOU ARE SO INNOCENT AND YOUR TECHNOLOGY IS SO SOPHISTICATED. I ALSO LOVE PARADOXES…AND INSECTS. COME, LET ME INTRODUCE YOU TO MY COLLEAGUES."

Tom and Petra were given a large top floor suite with a grand view, a car for touring, and an invitation each night to dine with Bunuel.

During the day, they swam in the thermal pools, took the sun, went up to their suite for some acrobatic sex and a nap, then touring in the rugged Michoacan mountains.

"Don't you feel like an idiot when he asks about his movies?" Petra said.

"Well, we can't lie," Tom said.

"I know that, but I feel like a philistine. Maybe we ought to ask to see one of his films."

"As long as the tickets are under two dollars," Tom laughed.

They didn't have to ask because their engaging, chainsmoking host had already arranged to show a subtitled version of one of his films.

"YOU KNOW, MY FRIENDS," he shouted after dinner, "I WAS BEGINNING TO LOSE INTEREST IN THE ACTUAL FILMING OF MY MOVIES UNTIL YOUR COMPANY DEVELOPED THAT DEVICE. THEN IT WAS AS IF I HAD A NEW PAIR OF EYES. FOR THAT, I'M DEEPLY GRATEFUL. TELL ME, WHAT ARE YOUR FAVORITE FILMS?"

Embarraassed again, Tom said, "We're not much on movies."

"LOOK AT THIS WONDERFUL INNOCENCE," Bunuel shouts. "YOU ARE PERFECT TO LOOK AT MY FILMS! BUT TELL ME, HAVE YOU NO MOVIE HISTORY AT ALL?"

"I find most movies unreal when they are trying to be real," Petra said tentatively.

Bunuel looked astonished. He motioned to his contingent to draw in closer as he paws his ear to listen more closely.

"PLEASE CONTINUE," he shouted, "CONTINUE."

"Petra has a word for it," Tom said.

"I think," she said, "they're not worth the price of admission."

"MY GOD!" Bunuel gasped.

Since Petra didn't know what that gasp meant, she stopped.

"I like Charley Chaplin films," Tom said, "and Petra likes a film called *The Enchanted Cottage.*"

"GET THAT FILM FOR ME!" Bunuel shouted at one of his assistants.

"MY DEAR TOM AND PETRA," he continued with a roar, "NOT ONLY HAVE YOU GRACED ME WITH YOUR PRESENCE, NOW I SEE YOU GRACE ME WITH YOUR

WISDOM. YOU ARE THE PERFECT AUDIENCE FOR MY FILMS."

"We are?"

"AND NOW LET ME EXTEND AN INVITATION TO YOU TO VISIT ME IN MEXICO CITY WHERE I LIVE WHILE I DO MY FILMING. I WOULD BE HONORED TO HAVE YOU AS MY GUESTS."

"Is it warm there?" Tom says.

"IT'S ALWAYS PLEASANT BUT NEVER HOT SINCE IT'S 8 THOUSAND FEET UP IN THE MOUNTAINS. YOU'VE NEVER BEEN THERE IN ALL THE TIME YOU'VE SPEND IN MEXICO?"

"No," Petra shouted, like an innocent.

"AND WHAT IS THE WORD?"

"The word?" Tom asked.

"THE WORD YOUR HUSBAND SAYS YOU HAVE FOR THE MOVIES."

Petra smiled and looked back and forth between her husband and the famous director.

'BULLSHIT!" she shouted.

Bunuel burst into laughter, rocking back and forth in his chair until it threatened to come apart.

In bed that night—oh, what a bed, what luxury!—naked and touching, Tom and Petra had a bit of an argument about going to Mexico City.

"You heard him," Petra said. "It's not hot there. If I'm on vacation, I want hot!"

"I know," Tom said, "but it's just for a few days. To visit him and see his work. He's famous. You liked the film, didn't you?"

"Yes, but I like what we do in the heat better."

"We have to move, Petra. We have to find a way to spend long winters down here."

"Or see a shrink," Petra said.

"You know what I'm thinking about right now?"

"What?"

"Maybe it was the movie. What was the name of it again?"

"*This Strange Passion*," Petra said.

"He said it had another title in Spanish."

"I cracked up about the guy's obsession with feet. What was his name?"

"Francisco."

"Just like me and my cold feet," Petra said. "Do you really think his obsession with feet was sexual? Are mine?"

"Definitely. For him, I mean. Did you see how he transfers his gaze from the priest kissing the boy's feet to the feet and legs of the woman he finally marries?"

"That was pretty funny."

"Surreal. Hilarious. Bunuel is a real mocker. Francisco had no idea he was sexually repressed. He couldn't admit his sexual tastes to himself and he ends up in this paranoid behavior."

"Do you think I'm sexually repressed?" Petra asked.

"Of course not," Tom said. "How can you say that?"

"I've got my hangups. My feet…."

"A hangup is not repression. This guy was a totally respectable man on the surface but a crazy pervert privately. Come on, Petra, he tries to sew up his wife's vagina."

"But we have to come to the tropics to have really great sex. Isn't that a kind of a fetish?"

"I would call it fetish-ini."

"Be serious," Petra said.

"We do all right in the summertime. It's those fucking cold winters. And we used to get by when my feet were always hot…"

"You were like toast."

"Not anymore," Tom said. "My feet are as cold as yours now."

"I know. Isn't it disgusting?"

"That film was wild." Tom said. "It made me think of all kinds of things. When I was a kid, a really small kid, I had trouble with my penis. I couldn't pull the skin back. Jesus, I haven't thought abot that in years."

"You never told me that."

"I never had the need to. It just popped into my head. I guess the doctor checked me and found I couldn't do it. He gave my mother some ointment to put on it…you know…to grease it…"

"You never told me about that," Petra repeated.

"Nobody ever told me," Tom said. "It was before my first hardon. I was just a little kid."

'So what happened?"

"It's not a secret I've kept from you. The crazy part was we were in the kitchen, my mother and I, I think my father was there, too, and she was trying to help me get the stuff on. I guess I was embarrassed. Here I am with my pants down around my ankles, I'm holding onto my penis, she's chasing me around and trying to be gentle. I'm hopping around the kitchen trying to escape while she's cooing and being as sweet as she can but I was just a kid and my penis hurt."

"Wow!" Petra said. "I read that sex is better when you're not circumcized."

"It's fine with me," Tom said. "So there I am and she's saying 'Just let me put a little on, Tommy, and then it will be better. There, there, it's going to be all better.'"

"And was it?"

"I didn't have any trouble after that. Hardons and all."

"I'll vouch for that," Petra said. "So why are you thinking about it now?"

"I don't know."

"Was it something in the movie?" Petra asked.

"I guess so. What do you think? I'm just wondering why we need all this heat. Maybe it isn't the heat."

"My cold feet are no illusion, Tom," Petra said.

"I know that, but if sex is all in the brain, then it's our brains. I mean, why is *The Enchanted Cottage* your favorite movie?"

"Because they love each other and everything in their ugly lives is transformed in their minds because of their love."

"Don't we love each other?" Tom said.

"Yes," Petra said.

"But you've got your shit at work and I've got my shit at work, then there's L.A. and all her misery….Don't you think it takes its toll?"

"It doesn't in the enchanted cottage," Petra said.

"That's because we didn't see them grow old. We just see them for a moment," Tom said. "And don't foreget your other favorite movie: Jon Hall and Maria Montez in *South of Pago Pago.*"

"I didn't want to mention it."

"Why not?"

"That's just for you and me to know about."

"But that explains the tropic."

Petra smiled and became misty and reflective.

"I always dreamed of making love under a waterfall, under a palm tree, in the turquoise water."

"We've gotten close," Tom said.

"But no cigar."

Tom felt insulted.

"You know what I mean," Petra said, tapping is chest with her slinky fingers.

"So are we going to Mexico City," Tom asked.

"Only if we spend most of our time on the hot torrid johnhallmariamontez coast," Petra said.

Chapter Eighteen

On summer afternoons—Saturdays, Sundays, weekdays—if he gets home early and the weather's good—Tom sits with his binoculars in the shade of his porch and looks out at the wetlands and up at the immense sky. He loves to look at clouds and their many shapes and moods. He loves to watch them change. He enjoys identifying the various profiles of human beings and animals the clouds take as the wind and breezes manipulate them. When he loses interest in the clouds because of uninteresting cloud cover, he lowers his binoculars to the wetlands and observes the birds and animals that make their home there. A distant roar then attracts his attention and he returns to the sky to watch planes on their flight paths to JFK airport. They have two flight paths, one over the ocean and one right over Tom's house. They come in at about eight thousand feet and Tom gets a kick out of being able to identify with his binoculars the details of the under carriages and the wheels as well as the particular name of the airline. Sometimes he cheats and makes the identification by the colors the planes are painted.

And then Tom rests his binoculars on his chest, closes his eyes, and thinks. There is much to think about, all on one subject: his daughter L.A. His first feeling is the all-too-familiar one: helplessness. Then agitation. Then anger. And then a confused troop of other feelings, all distinguishable, all biting and vexatious. She was provocative from the first moments of her life but in the past six years the provocations have turned to unalloyed pain.

Her younger brother and sister, G.C. and K.A., sometimes get lost in the turmoil and Tom has to make a special effort to keep in touch with their lives, irrespective of their connection to their troubled sister—G.C, in his world, K.A. in hers.

What would have happened if she never met Phil? Never laid eyes on him? Never got introduced to him by his brother Donald who was sweet on her? She worked at Orange Julius in the Mall. There she met Donald and there she met Phil who was the manager of the Mall's health food store. If Donald was friendly, personable and charming, Phil was aggressive, driven, and entirely in charge of all situations he found himself in. So he believed. When he saw L.A. for the first time—her blond hair swept up uder the Orange Julius cap, making her startling brown eyes even more vivid and beautiful—her decided that this prettiet of girls would be his.

This is how Tom has come to understand the beginning of what turned out to be the tragedy of young life. She was swept off her feet by a powerful surge of maleness, of spunk, of color, of appearances. Phil wore the best and most fashionable of clothes, the drove the niftiest car, he sent her roses by the dozens, he called her incessantly, he remembered every detail of conversation, he weas never at a loss. He was fast and slick and it all came across to Tom as acceptable, even as personable. Here was a younf man with ambition. Good. That would make up for what he saw was lacking in his own children.

Even though he was only in his early twenties, Phil's plans were already made. He was going to become rich in the health food business. Managership of the Mall store was just the beginning. Once he knew the business inside out he was going to open his own and soon there was going to be a chain of stores and then money, houses, clothes, and bars. Oh, yes, bars, the latest, the fastest, the flashiest, the most exotic. It was written that way. There was no doubt about it and L.A. would have it all with him.

Tom picks up his binoculars and watches a crane or heron land not a hundred feet from him, just at the edge of the wet lands. The crane stands tentatively, listening, looking, deciding: Is this safe? Shall I stay here? Whar are the dangers? His dark eyes, his thin frame, his long beak reflect a nervousness, an anticipation of peril. He is never at ease.

Tom liked Phil, Petra was noncommital. Now they pillory themselves, Tom for his blindness, Petra from her silence.

"I'll never keep my mouth shut again," Petra says.

"Why did you in the first place?" Tom asks.

"I didn't want to interfere in her life. What good would it have done if I told her how I really felt? She was in love with him. I just told her one thing. I asked her if she felt her love rigfht down to her toes, the way I did with you. She said she didn't know. That was the key. What could I tell her—to feel like I do? I told her what I knew."

"I liked him," Tom says. "I really liked him. He could see I wasn't behaving like the usual protective father and he wondered about it. How many times did her tell me I'm from Mars? He'd look at all the books and music in our house and wonder what I was doing in manufacturing. Why hadn't I become a professor? He caught all the nuances of our lives. Maybe that's why I couldn't see through him."

"I did," Petra says, "but I decided to say nothing.

"Not even to me. Why?"

"I don't know. Maybe I was afraid of imposing on her the way my family imposed on me. I don't know. I wanted her to make her own choices. I just can't believe that my daughter would make such a terrible error."

"What are we supposed to take from this?" Tom says. "That we should have been autocratic? that we should have imposed our will on her?"

"She would have rebelled more than she did."

"We aided in her rebellion," Tom says, "and the fact is she didn't know what she was doing. But how couldn't she know what she was doing? She came from a sane and sensible family, we set a good example, there was no dishonesty in our house."

"Maybe there was too much protection," Petra says.

"But was there? We were open, we were uptodate, we were reasonable. That's what disturbs me so much. This teaches me that reason and even love don't go very far when they come up against guile and manipulation and cunning. That's the terrible lesson of Phil Lopes in our lives."

"Amnd yet if Phil were listening to this, he wouldn't recognize himself."

"Recognize himself," Tom says. "He'd protest vehemently. He would tell us we've got it all wrong, it's L.A.'s fault, he's the victim. I'll never forget the weeping he did on our porch— how many times have I told you? I can't get it out of my head. I've never seen a man cry the way Phil cried, and there I was sympathizing with him, stroking his head, patting his shoulder while he wept and told my of my daughter's infidelities—while he was fucking every woman or girl he could get his hands on. It's almost demonic—the whole thing!"

"But that was different," Petra said sarcastically.

"I had never met anyone like this—I was fifty years old and I had never met anyone like him. What does that say about me?"

"He always said you were from Mars," Petra says.

"That I couldn't see through his deceit? But he doesn't see his own deceit. He's the victim."

"The only victim."

What Tom hides from Petra is too painful to admit. He thinks he pushed L.A. into Phil'a grip. He was eager to get his difficult daughter out of the house and she was eager to go. He pushed, he permitted. Petra said nothing. Based on the order in their lives – the normalcy—he assumed things would turn out for the best.

L.A. wen to live with Phil and soon Tom felt he had a second son. They had Sunday dinners together, they spent the big holidays together, they sepnt summers at the beach together and L.A. seemed to begin to enjoy her family more than ever. Or so it seemed.

Tom recalls a look on L.A.'s face; he'd seen it often. He thought to meant she was pleased that Phil and her father were getting along. But now he knows differently. That expression— one he'll never forget—had a far different meaning. It now tells of her confusion, her conflict, her trap. It says, "How come I can't get along with him but everybody else can? Look how affectionately he and my father behave toward one another. How well he gets along with everyone else in the family; even Mom. So it must be me. I'm the one who makes life miserable because of my hostile and angry personality. And then Phil retaliates. I'm being treated hop I deserve to be treated."

Phil followed through on his stated ambitions. With a loan from his parents, he opened a stor with Donald in a high density spot near the University and had instant success. Only two years later they opened a second one but they were too confident of their selling skills and too hasty about the location and it failed. Donald bailed out, took his girlfriend and went to Colorado, leaving Phil in need of trusted assistants. Quite naturally he turned to the Amphibologies. He employed K.A. and G.C. taught them the business and let them run it for him while he went to college to get his degree and catch up with L.A. Tom saw nothing in this but good omens. A good mix of styles and personalities was producing excellent results all around. He wanted all of his children to have college educations and he succeeded at that, but all three were strongly wanting in ambition. Phil came along, a young man—if Tom wanted to ber harsh—from the other side of the tracks, hiding his Puerto Rican background behind European Spanish ancestry and making sure that his surname was pronounced as one syllable rather than two so that it carried not the least trait of derided origins. This young man was nothing if not ambitious and when he realized he was the only member of his new family without a college education, he took immediate steps to correct his shortcoming. Wit the support and assistance of his future father-in-law, Phil completed undergraduate studies in three and a half years with a major in history. Tom applauded him and when the burdens and pressures of business and education became too great he pitched in to assist Phil directly by writing papers for him and reading books for him. Phil even took a trip with Tom to see the boiling vats of New Jersey, something that G.C. would never do. For Tom, Phil was providing his children with a spark that was needed to ignite and propel them into action. It hadn't come from him and Petra.

The store prospered. Phil had degrees, and now he was talking about law school. But first marriage. Phil and L.A.'s first arguments in front of Tom and Petra were about the kind of wedding it would be. L.A. wanted a small unconventional wedding down at the beach, her favorite palce for sun and sea and sand. Phil wanted a perfectly conventional wedding that all of his friends and neighbors from the old neighborhood could attend. L.A. won out, but at a price. Phil was unhappy and she was in a poor mood prior to the wedding. IT was at that time that Petra asked her if she were sure of herself. L.A.'s answer did not inspire Petra with confidence, but so much of their lives were already so different that Petra did not know where to begin her belated guidance.

The marriage ceremony and reception were successful and since they were already living together, L.A. and Phil resumed the normal course of their lives very quickly after to honeymoon. It was then that Petra began to notice occasional marks on L.A.'s arms. She questioned her about them and L.A. told her she was a klutz and was continually banging into things. Having no reason to think the cause of the bruises was any different, Petra didn't mention them to Tom. Then while Phil was opening a second and this time more successful store in another town, L.A. became pregnant. That joy was accompanied by K.A.'s partnership with Phil in the second store. She had collected ten thousand dollars in an accident case and invested it all with Phil.

When summer came L.A. was in her sixth month and was extremely moody. Every weekend Phil begged her to go out to Montauk with him and every weekend she refused. On both Saturday and Sunday mornings Phil, being an excellent surfer, left esrly to "catch the waves." In a terrible mood, L.A. went ovet to her parents' for company. When Tom questioned why she didn't go with Phil, she let her pregnancy answer for her. And when she needed further arguments, given her excellent health, Petra supplied them.

"Can't she go even once?" Tom asked Petra.

"Can't he stay home with his pregnant wife—even once?" Petra retorted.

Tom was disappointed with his daughter. It seemed to him she was withdrawing. Was the pregnancy doing that to her? When he tried to raise the subject with her, she drove him off with moodiness and hostility –the same expresions of inner discontent he had long been familiar with and hoped would come to an end with marriage and maturity.

Chapter Nineteen

Tom oesn't like to think bout politics too much, and doesn't like the century he's living in.

This is what politics and the history of the twentieth century has done to him.

When he looks at and reads about the violent history of his century, he feels the shame of a survivor, the helplessness of the conscience-stricken affluent.

But since he has never experienced any of the violence of the century, his emotions have curdled within him. He has escaped by dumb luck and sheer chance when so mnay of hundreds of millions of murdered human being have not been able to.

As far as he knows, nobody else feels the way he does. He has come to this conclusion because he has tested people, he's asked them questions, he's probed, and he's been rebuffed. He meets indifference, he meets coldness, meets calculatingness. He concludes he's somewhere off in left field in these matters, he doesn't know how to let go and let pass and he doesn't understand how the world works, its power politics, its geopolitics, its lunapolitics, or any politics. And yet, watching tv and reading, he absorbs politics more than anything else. As a result he has won the tv set from Petra (a Pyrrhic victory) who will not watch it anymore if Tom persists in watching only new and politics, and sports, of course.

"Can't we find a nice story to watch?" Petra says from time to time after snuggling up to him on the couch. "Just a nice story about some interesting people."

Tom give her the monitor and says, "Find it," knowing that Petra is a harsher critic of tv material than he is. Inside of five minutes, she is flicking through the channels faster than Tom does when he's bored with the tube.

"What shit!" she shrieks. She throws the monitor at him and leaves the room. "I've got ironing to do anyway."

After dinner Tomn always watches McNeil-Lehrer, Crossfire, and then tunes into CNN and C-Span. He has been watching these programs for much of his adult life and while he is well-informed intellectually, his curled feeligs have not changed. Here is his life, there are those problems. Nothing matches. The gap between him and the Palestinian problem, or Apartheid, or guerrilla warfare, or perversions of human rights, or homelessness, or poverty and famine is so wide that he spins into the gap instead of trying to bridge it. It is all an intellectual exercise and schizoid emotional consequences.

He blames his collapse on the Kennedy years. At least the beginning of it. The shock of the Kennedy assassination should have been a signal of the troubles to come. American presidents and world leaders have been assassinated throughout history, Tom knew it, but the media has hoisted Kenndey to such mythological heights (Camelot, when in truth he came a lot) that his fall was bound to shatter the nation. Tom, too. Then came the coverup investigations and the concealment of documents not to be opened til any Kennedy is long dead. Following that, the revelations about Kennedy's bogus family life and active sex life in the White House killed off the remainder of the illusions. But all that was just the beginning.

Then came Johnson's lying intentions about Vietnam and the trut about secret governance. When knowledge fo the two governments became clear to Tom, the curdle in him froze. The roll call of disastrous leadership and monumental lying following Kennedy drummed a permanent cynicism into Tom. Johnson, Vietnam; Nixon, Watergate, and Resignation under the threat of Impeachment; Reagan, Grenada, Panama, Nicaragua, El Salvador, the Iran-Contra Hearings, the S and L scandals, Bush and The Persian Gulf all became versions of American imperialism which the American government had worked vigorously to conceal from The American people. Tom concluded that the American people can't face, can't confront, can't handle the fact of American imperial power and imperial design and won't send its sons and daughters to war under those auspicies, the American government must conceal its motives and thereby always be out of touch with its citizens. Another version of Catch-22. If the American government wants to be in touch with its citizens, then it must tell the truth about its intentions. In telling the truth, it will lose the support of its citizens and worse, not be able to get their sons and daughters to fight for its imperial designs. So when the Persian Gulf War came along, the most monumental propaganda campaign in modern history had to be mounted, lie after relentless lie had to be fabricated and told until Americans believed that their freedoms were somehow at stake and that they had to fight a new Hitler or they would not survive. That campaign was further proof that there are two governments—one the people believed in, which existed only in their minds, and one that was actually there—the imperial superpower.

Tom hates to be lied to, hates his country to be the victimizer, but there it is. It sits heavily on his mind and causes him to hate the century he is living in while he likes the life he is living in the century he hates living in. So much for McNeil-Lehrer, Crossfire, CNN, C-Span.

Tom doesn't know what to do with all of this, so it just lays on his brain like week-old egg. Isn't everybody, isn't Tom better off watching Jeopardy, not knowing or feeling any of this? And yet he doesn't see any faces looking any happier than his.

Chapter Twenty

Tom's gut has disappeared. That's discipline. It's taken months of daily walking, aerobic exercise, reduction of calories, and less fat intake. Tra-la! Voila! His gut is flat. He's juft 13 pounds heavier than he was as a skinny 25 year old.

He and Petra ftand naked together, side by side, before the day of judgment wall-to-wall mirrors in the bathroom and ooh and ahh over each other's shape.

"How many old farts can do this without wanting to jump out the window?" Tom says.

"And do you know what it saves on clothes?" Petra says. "Some of my things are years old but I can still wear them although I'm going to throw that blue dress out even though it still fits. It embarrasses me it's so ancient."

"Just think, Petra," Tom says, "these are almost our same bodies as they were thirty years ago. The look of them…."

"Well, I wouldn't got that far," Petra says. "My legs could be a lot better, and I have to struggle with this stomach."

"My whole shape could be a lot better," Tom says, "I don't have enough of a waist, but I'm talking about what we started with."

Standing side by side, the hold hands and look and are proud. No major scars, no surgeries, no bulges, no limp hanging fat, no rolls of excessive flesh. A male and a female.

"Three children came out of you," Tom says. "Remember how big you got with each one?"

"I was an elephant—three times."

"And out came three big ones."

"And L.A. was the biggest problem. She didn't want to be born. They had to cut me. Boy, did Dr. Murray sweat! He didn't expect any trouble."

"Do you think L.A. was born for trouble?"

"I don't know."

"I never believed that temperament could be such a factor," Tom said, "but she changed my mind."

"She's taught us all a thing or two," Petra says.

"And K.A. and G.C.?"

"Different temperaments."

"She was first born."

"Remember how she cried."

"Weeks and weeks."

"She had her nights and days confused."

"Remember eating dinner with her on the table. She always wanted company."

"Maybe we were too easy with her."

"How long could we let her cry? We tried it once and she threw up."

"I never thought that life was a mystery," Tom says, "but that's what she taught me."

"She's a wonderful giving person."

"That's one side of her, but there's the other and when that side of her clashed head on with Phil….Do you remember when we conceived her? What was going on?"

"What do you mean?

"Between us."

"We were living in Brooklyn, we decded to have a baby and we did."

"Were you having an affair?" Tom asks.

"Oh yeah! Were you?"

"With the IRT. Remember? Two jobs."

"She said to me the other day—crying— 'it's not supposed to be this way.'"

"I've never seen anybody shed so many tears," Tom says. "Sometimes I think she's used up the world's supply. You used to cry like that."

"I did not."

"You don't remember? I do. Sometimes you scared me."

"You were easily scared then. I just want her to be happy," Petra says, "and I never see her happy."

Petra shivers.

"I'm getting cold."

"Let's put some clothes on," Tom says.

Chapter Twenty-One

Tom and Petra decide to move. Their children are gone, more than less on their own. Why then do Tom and Petra need such a big house? They are getting older and they gasp when they think of the energy they expended on work, family, home, and grounds. Now they have new horizons. They are going to spread their wings. This is not as easy as it sounds for reasons I will expand upon in a while. But first let Tom and Petra take a trip down memory lane. They do this from time to time, sometimes in bed, sometimes in the car, sometimes over breakfast or dinner when one of them reads something that kindles long memories.

Tom reads an article about the Dutch fetish for cleanliness. Householders in that tiny country on the North Sea are continually sweeping their streets, cleaning their houses, scrubbing, polishing, and dusting. And then in springtime they turn their houses upside down for a knockdowen, drag-out two week purification. This obsession with cleanliness has something to do with their Calvinist heritage which has taught them the value of godliness and personal responsibility.

Tom knows a little bit about how Holland, part of which exists below sea level, ruled sea trade for a couple of hundred years and left colonies all over the world. There's evidence of it close by in New York City with its Dutch names like Brooklyn, Van Cortlandt, Bleecker, Great Kills, New Dorp, Amsterdam, Paerdegat, Styvesant, and Harlem. And there's the famous Dutch Reformed Protestant Church in Flatbush right near where Tom was born and grew up.

"After all those years o cleaning morning til night, I can't bring myself to do any more of it," Petra says guiltily.

"Well, I pick up the slack," Tom says, who is good at floors, bathrooms, and rugs. Especially bathrooms. He is great at bathrooms. He calls himself 'The Shithouse King.'

"You're good," Petra says, "but you don't dust."

"I hate dusting," Tom says, "but I do everything else."

"That's true," Petra says. "You're good."

He even cooks.

But the fact is that nobody cleans like Petra in the old days when she had phenomenal energy.

"I would start when the kids went off to school and not finish til midnight."

"Don't I know it," Tom says. "Your cleaning got in the way of our sex life."

"It did. I din't remember you saying that."

"I didn't. I was consumed with my own senseless projects. Sex is much better since we're older and relaxed. Wouldn't you say?"

Petra is a bit coy, but she nods.

"Didn't you say that the best sex we ever has was between forty-five and fifty-five?" Tom says.

Petra smiles and nods.

"That's true….it's still good," she quickly adds, "but not quite as…."

"Spectacular?" Tom throws in.

"Well…" she says.

"Do you think there's a connection between cleanliness and sex?"

"Like what?"

"The more you clean, the less sex. Do you think it's true of the Dutch?"

"Pass the sugar, Mr. Freud," Petra says.

"Sex isn't clean, is it?" Tom says.

"What are you talking about?"

"Look at the dirty things we do."

"Dirty?"

"Well, you know, we wouldn't do them in the street, would we?"

"You would," she says.

"We have to conceal them from the sight of others. We have to get rid of the evidence."

"First you're wild, then you're not."

"I gues I am," Tom says as they both trail off into their papers.

Petra's the one who forces the issue on WORLD WIDE TRAVEL!! Until now, she and Tom have done a little traveling: a couple of weeks in the Caribbean every years, once to Mexico, a your have read. The Caribbean has become their backyard, so to speak. Actually there's a great big story there. There's always a story because Tom had a fear of flying even though he had been in the Air Force. (Figure that one out.) If you really want to know, read his novel called *His Father's Son* which he wanted to call *The Volunteer* but Petra nixed that one. Were they going to be stuck on Long Island the rest of their lives, Petra wanted to know, or was Tom going to do something about it? He thought about it. Petra's right, he said and so with Petra's help did do something about it but it wasn't easy. You see, Tom's always been a homeboy. He loves his books, he loves poking around his library, he loves terra firma. Petra want to see things. She wants experience. Since Tom didn't want to disappoint his lovely wife, he made an appointment ar Kennedy Airport to inspwct a jet, to get to know it, to confront his fear, get comfortable with it. It was easy to do because it was the 1970s and airport security was very loose at that time. When he got to the airport with Petra and three children and met a very pleasant pilot, Tom told him his wife had a terrible fear of flying, could he show her the inside of the jet because she was also claustrophobic, didn't like the idea of being shut up inside a cigar? The pilot was sympathetic and escorted the whole family onto the plane. While he familiarized Petra and the kids with the interior of the jet, Tom was free to examine and explore and feel and react. HE checked the seating, he checked the toilets, he checked the overhead bins, he checked the breathing room, he checked the space he would have to himself. Back and forth, he walked the length of the plane. He recalled flying in an Air Force transport plane with the exit door open and the cold wind rushing at him, swirling across his face. He gasped at the thousands of feet of air between him and the ground and he felt a fear that drew him to the open door. He held onto the bulkhead of the naked interior of that transport. Was something drawing him to that open door? That was the beginning of it all. Could he overcome that fear?

Petra and the kids played their parts well. They thanked the pilot profusely and the pilot responded with a salute. HE looked at Tom with a wink and Tom winked back. They understood how it was with women.

When they got home Tom and Petra made two lists. The had found this technique in a psychology book. You take a piece of paper and divide it down the middle. You label one side "Reality" and the other "Imagination" or "Fantasy". On the "Reality" side you list all the horrible things that could happen to the plane. That list turned out to be very short. The plane could crash and you could be killed or badly injured. The list on the "Imagination" side was very long. The mind weaves, invents, capitulates to emotion, to phobias, to myths, to rumor, to dreams. Tom concluded it's simple. He understood the reality. The rest is fantasy.

And so Tom and Petra began flying to the Caribbean but it wasn't easy for Tom. He gritted his teeth and tried to calm his quaking heart. (A pill ot two helped.) He did it because he loved the Caribbean and he loved Petra in the Caribbean where color and light exploded in your face, entered your bones, filled you with a roused senses. He could not bear to surrender all that beauty to his fears. It took six flights for Tom to relax a bit.

And now Petra says, "Let's spread out wings! I want to see things. We've got the money, we've got our health, let's go!"

"Where to?" Tom says.

"Everywhere!" Petra says. "I don't want to end up on a couch with a comforter on my knees watching some idiotic television program while I nod off. Let's go!"

And so they are going, have gone, will go.

Tom renamed Petra. He now calls her Marco Polo.

Chapter Twenty-Two

For ten years Tom and Petra traveled the world, traveled around the world, traveled in the world, traveled through the world, not all at once but in stages carefully planned and executed by the one and only Petra Amphibologies, aka Marco Polo.

Tom was be reading in his favorite spot besides the bedroom, the den. It was the poetry of G. Apollinaire, wounded in W W I and never the same, dead from flu epidemic at 37, author of *Zone* and *Calligrammes* (Pictuer Words), etc. Petra sat down next to him with pen and paper and pen and engaged his attention away from his serious reading. She, having learned to be prepared with any proposal, outlined an extensive travel program which they could well afford. Tom, though not as excited as Petra about the prospect of travel, fully agreed with her plans. He loved Petra and what made her happy, made him happy. He was aware that domesticity while satisfying did not fulfill her and here were opportunities to break free. They were retired now and the world, as they say, awaited them.

So off they went, in stages, over ten years to: Italy (twice) France (twice) Switzerland, Austria, The Low Countries, Hong Kong, Thailand, Australia, New Zealand, Costa Rica, Guatemala, Cayman Islands, and their beloved Caribbean where they had vacationed years before the light bulb went off in Petra's lively mind. Their Caribbean travels had been small change compared to Petra's new big plans.

They landed in an Alitalia 747 at Rome's Leonardo de Vinci airport which was as good as first class, clean, shipshape. Petra immediately noticed that Romans were much more stylish dressers than Americans. (Americans: no style.)

Then they flew an hour north to Venice which was damp, chilly, overcast and overrated. Petra said she couldn't wait for warm Sicily. But there they were in Piazza San Marco and all the churches, squares, bridges and gondolas which zipped carelessly through the canals. Tom couldn't avoid talking about the graffiti, garbage, power plants, cranes, and the instability of being surrounded and inundated by invasive waters, even up to the hotel's doorstep. Regarding the graffiti, some of it slashed on walls said, in Italian, of course, which Tom made sure to have translated: "Blacks, Go Home" "Fascists Eat Dead Bodies." Petra warned Tom to be in vacation mode but he couldn't help recalling Robert Benchley's remark in a telegram home: "Wonderful city! Streets full of water. Please advise."

Venice was to be the first stop on their Italian journey which would lead them down the boot to the very edges and interiors of triangular-shaped Sicily. Lots of water around in Venice. They met their tour mates and handsome guide Franco Falanga at the classy Bauer-Grunwald Hotel and, after breakfast, were all set to go! One of their stops was at the glass blowers called Special Murano. Tom and Petra were fascinated at the magic and skill of making glass. Of course Petra bought a small Venetian cranberry wine glass. (She loved cranberry.) It was priced at 640,000 lire but she got it for 600. ($400 from her stash.) When they got back to the hotel, Petra opened the carefully filled and sealed box to make sure Murano didn't switch glasses or try to fake her out in some other way. (Shrewd Petra.) But they didn't.

After putting the sacred and expensive cranberry Murano wine glass in the box and resealing it, Tom and Petra— she walking faster than he— went off to the Rialto business district and got lost. After meandering through narrow, rainy streets, Petra spotted a glass seller and went in to price the Murano cranberry glass. They met Roberta, a sales agent and asked her price for the wine glass. She said the equivalent of $317 and could do even better. Petra saw red, not cranberry. They went looking further and the wine glass at Pauly's went for $122, a little scratched. Petra saw redder with rising fury. They found their way back to the first agent, Enrico Minuti (Tom, more interested in geography than glass, discovered he was from Messina, Sicily). Enrico listened cooly and held to his price. Petra fretted about a swindle but took Enrico's advice to go home, think about it, and return after 3:30 to talk to his manager. On the way back to the hotel, Tom and Petra stopped at Roberta's and asked for her boss. He was Roberto, the owner, who spoke English as well as Tom and Petra. Blue-eyed and handsome, he was a born-and-bred Venetian. What made Tom laugh and Petra smile just a bit was Roberto's description of Byzantine business dealing in Byzantine Venice.

`"Nothing," he told them, "is real. Venice isn't real, it's a grown-up's Disneyland and has been from the beginning. Venice has stood still for hundreds of years instead of developing. All it's good for now is tourism. The city is dying. There are no children, only old people so I'll tell you what: you're wasting your time trying to bargain in Venice. Why don't you keep the one you bought and I'll sell you one for $200 and you'll have two for $600. You'll have a real bargain."

"Petra said, "No thanks," and they went off to see Enrico but like everywhere else they experienced in Venice—including their room at the famous hotel—they got lost. And their room kept evading them because it was 222 but it was on the third floor, or at least floor two and a half.

They hunted for Murano's glassblowers and factory and that also evaded them for three-quarters of an hour. They asked directions and were misdirected twice but they got to Enrico about 3:30 who shrugged and suggested there was nothing to be done.

"Do you intend to return it?" he asked.

"Yes," Petra said.

"Then all right, I'll call the manager."

He came out, saw Petra's conviction, passed Tom a benign slur, and said he'd give it to them for $300.

Petra gave in because she really wanted a cranberry wine glass which she had marked for a spot among her cranberry things at home on the mantle.

Meanwhile, the hotel flooded which was a unique experience for May, said one of the Bauer-Grunwald staff.

The weather continued to be awful but cleared for Petra and Tom's gondola ride on the Grand Canal which included an accordion player and a singer with a beautiful voice. His heartfelt and melodious singing made Venice come alive.

Then thunder, more rain, and flood.

They were relieved to be getting out of cold Venice even though it was a pleasure sitting in San Marco Piazza thinking themselves into a scene of the movie *Summertime* with Katherine Hepburn about to meet Rosanno Brazzi.

It was a long winding bus trip to Firenze (Florence for you Americans) Italy is so mountainous there was no straight roads, but the scenery is breathtaking. Nevertheless, Tom with his sensitive stomach was nauseous when they got to the hotel. He sent Petra off on the Santa Croce trip alone (with the group, of course), where she, an alluring woman, was 'approached'. This is how she told it:

"I wanted a leather jacket and stopped into a leather goods store. And I found it. I always wanted a leather jacket and here it was. I has helped by a tall Italian (of course) who was wearing a leather jacket. He helped me in and out of a couple of them and then as I bought it—you won't believe this, Tom—he asked me out to dinner."

"Out to dinner?"

"Yes," Petra said with an approving smile.

"Wha'd you do?"

"Well, I smiled at him…."

"Of course."

"..and said 'I'm married', and he said, 'What has that got to do with a lovely dinner.'"

"Holy cow, Petra."

"I thanked him, left the store and joined the group."

"That's the last time I let you out alone," Tom said. "Especially in Italy." But Tom was proud of Petra, proud that she was his.

In Firenze it was the Academy, San Lorenzo Church, Il Duomo, Pitti Palace, the Uffici Palace (Offices, that's all, but how profound in Italian!), art, art and more art—Botticelli, Giotto, Raphael, Michelangelo, and then the fruit stores, lunch at

American Express: a bottle of wine, salad, bread, ribollito soup, minestrone soup, dessert and caffe' and Tom's delight in Petra's company. And then Siena, beautiful, classy, medieval, handsome; and St. Catherine's head and finger—all a wonder including in one small square which housed three buildings: one Gothic, one Renaissance, one Mannerist— 13th, 14th, and 15th centuries. And the old city with its hilly streets, steep and narrow.

With the weather still chilly, they left for Rome, a long wearying ride through lovely countryside, Petra allegry-suffering, and then, eventually, Rome on a sunny warming day and then the Colosseum, Moses, Fountain of Trevi, 'The Birthday Cake', the Spanish Steps, the Roman Forum, the crazy traffic, the chaos, anarchist graffiti. And more churches. Petra said that the monuments of ancient Rome and the overpowering presence of the Catholic Church made her feel small; they humbled her. Tom said they were supposed to be; that's why they were built. But Rome is warmer in all senses: weather, people, atmosphere, Petra complaining of exhaustion but zinging along. And then Hadrian's Villa and Tivoli, Villa D'Este, Borghese Gardens, and more graffiti: Fuck the Police, No Nato, Capitalismo e' Babaro, D.C. Assassina, Morte a' Zingari, Palestina Libera, Italia Libera....

Chapter Twenty-Three

Rome to Sorrento with Domenico the driver and Franco, the smooth, dapper Sorrentino. Naples and its bay a disappointment to Tom and Petra because of the smog, fog or mist depending on who describes it. Franco called it mist. The bay was socked in and Vesuvius foggy. The Med looked clear but "the Carib beats this out," Petra said, "but not the steep cliffs to the water," Tom added, and the three hundred foot climb to the hotel—The Grand Vesuvio Hotel. The Sorrento sun was hot and Tom and Petra soaked it up on their patio. The hotel itself seemed a strange-looking place, Tom felt, all marble, sort of Art Deco with conflicting tones of coldness and bareness, even barrenness. It looked unfinished, inside and out. Maybe because it wasn't the summer season.

Franco was pessimistic and the future of Italy. Cost of living was high, gas was five dollars a gallon, the youth wasn't being educated to compete in the European Union, money was in the hands of the few and "there are no geniuses around."

They walked down the hill to Sorrento, walked around, exchanged money, looked for the bus stop at Antico Muro and couldn't find it. Patra was unhappy and blamed Tom for going the wrong way. But the views from the hills were terrific.

They had lunch at an outdoor restaurant and ate the worst pizza they ever tasted, salty and board-like. But Sorrento was pretty much what all the songs say it is: oranges, Lemon trees, flowers, scenery and the slow pace. Siesta time is one-thirty to three-thirty.

They sailed to Capri which was warm and sunny and congested but lovely, anyway; then the scenic wonders, the funicular, the ride to Anacapri, more views, sunny scenic splendors, gardens, a monument to Lenin who stayed a while.... a former house of the Krupp family....

Back in Sorrento, Franco took Tom and Petra and a small group to his buddy's restaurant called Il Mulino where they had a fine dinner in an outdoor area filled with flowers and plants and the day's warmth. It was European dining—plenty of time and many courses, music and conversation. Then they walked to the Tasso Square where Sorrentinos socialize. It was lovely. Tom reflected that America loses badly on many counts by comparison. Italians were wonerfully alive, warm, expressive, loving, crazy drivers, yes, but they really do watch where they are going Franco told him. Chaotic but not dangerous. And the further south Tom and Petra went, the better it got—oranges, lemons, grapes, olives, lush foliage, and the sun!

Sicily! Finally!

Tom and Petra left Sorrento sadly at 8, got on the ferry to Villa San Giovanni about 4 pm, Messina is just two miles but twenty minutes by Ferry.

Franco said that the south of Italy is nowhere.

"You can survive here but there are few motivations to stay put. You are born here and come here to die, but in between you head out—north or Anerica—to make some money."

Petra, having some roots in Sicily, was disappointed on the region from Messina to Taormina—dry unkempt, and begging gypsies right off the ferry, everything looking rundown.

As they approached Taormina they saw some beautiful sights although the town at sea level was tacky. The Hotel Alfio was a beauty, having the appearance of a Roman Villa with pretty gardens and pool and a lovely dining room. Their room was smallish, but okay, with a small balcony from which they could view the Ionian Sea. Mt. Etna loomed thirty miles away.

Dinner in the lovely blue and white dining room was a bit on the peculiar side for Tom and Petra nutrititonal tastes: bean soup, macaroni, potatotes, veal, spinach with butter and heavy desserts. And the water "non potabile". So it was bottled, but not the wine.

In their room there was Pagine Gialle Turismo (Yellow Pages for Tourists), outdated by a couple of years. The front part was full of ads and info; the back had the ywllow pages. The info about Sicily was the frankest and openest and bluntest Tom and Petra ever encountered. There was poetry, a discussion of Sicilian literature and a frank, not to say depressing, exposure of real Sicilian temperaments. "An island of writers," it said, "from inferno to spring." And Sicily was described as a people on its knees, and the Sicilians as losers. Bracing but strange.

Then, after Petra bought a beautiful pain of leather sandals in Taormima, onto Teatro Greco with guide Pina. Built by the Greeks (not Pina but she did have beautiful eyes) and made over three times: Greeks, Romans (twice) up to 200 B.C. Pina re-enforced the view we read on Tourist Yellow Pages. She said Sicilians feel victimized. They want to leave but are ashamed of saying they are Sicilians. They deny their heritage, say they are mainly Greek rather than Italian. The southern coast of Sicily is called "The African Coast." She recommended Sicilian authors: Di Roberto, Verga, Sciascia, Lampedusa, Bufalino. Di Roberto's book is called *The Vice Kings*.

Petra said the country is beautiful and magnificent—the antiquity, the art, the natural beauty. All overwhelming. The down side of the trip was the fast moving around: Two days here, three days there, packing, unpacking, on the road too much. One night, after going off to sleep after a walk in town and a cappucino, bombs started going off with great and even louder regularity. They were Italian fireworks which sounded very different from American fireworks. It was all in honor of some saint, so Tom and Petra decided to make their own fireworks, sixty-two and sixty-four year-old variety.

Siracusa was hot where they visited a Greek theater and a Roman theater and were shown the differences.

Chapter Twenty-Four

Tom and Petra had few close friends. It had always been that way. One could say they lived in a personal cocoon, satisfied with themselves, their family and few others of any duration. Living all their lives on Long Island, they had moved around a bit: from Brooklyn to Huntington, to Port Jeff Station, to Setauket on the north shore, to Moriches on the south shore, and a timeshare at Gurney's Inn in Montauk. That's a bit of changing and moving for the short stretch of Long Island, a mere 120 miles long.

Tom taught in three school districts in three different towns and Petra, once Tom retired, went into the business world. As a result, Tom became a househusband (domestic tasks of which he enjoyed; it also gave him a lot of time to write) and Petra brought home the bacon, as it were. It was a fine arrangement, satisfying both of them.

Along the way, they met only one couple who stuck to them, and not very closely or intimately until.......But let's not jump ahead too quickly.

In one school district Tom met Jim, a history teacher. (Tom taught English.) Jim happened to want to be a writer and when he found out that Tom had already written a few novels, they struck up a relationship, sharing their work. Tom was welcoming about Jim's ambition and did what he could to encourage him. He lent Jim a completed manuscript of a novel and subsequent to that Jim gave Tom parts of a tentative novel, or a work-in-progress. Tom liked it and encouraged Jim to finish it. Jim was gratified by Tom's criticism and support; and soon went on the finish the novel. By this time, Tom, Jim, and Petra were friends. Jim then revealed that he was having an affair with a math teacher in the school and soon Adrienne, the math teacher, became part of the small group. All four were agreeable and convivial and spent occasional evenings together, or went out to dinner filling their time together with lively conversation. At the same time Jim and Adrienne's personal lives, which were complex, came out in the open. Tom and Petra were smug in their cocoon while Jim and Adrienne were struggling in a number of ways while using Tom and Petra as their sounding board.

Adrienne was divorced and had a teen-aged son. Jim, too, was divorced and had a teen-aged daughter. Their former spouses were often a topic of denigrating conversation. While Adrienne expressed contempt for her former husband, Jim said he only married Thelma because she was pregnant. It was the honorable thing to do but there was nothing else of value in the relationship. The marriage then disintegrated quickly. In his novels, Jim stayed away from his personal life and focused on historical subjects which he did well, according to Tom. Petra did not read them. Over the years they shared their enthusiasm over each others' work but the commercial markets had different ideas about what was publishable and they both were not successful.

As time went on Jim and Adrienne began to describe their own conflicts with each other. They expressed love for one another but Jim was seeing other women which disturbed Adrienne. At the same time their sex life was very active and supremely satisfying to her, she having been disappointed in her earlier marriage. She did not like Jim's behavior with other women but she balanced that with her own need of him. Not only did they discuss this openly with Tom and Petra, Jim and Adrienne used to settle their arguments on Tom and Petra's couch. After describing their differences they did everthing on the couch but make physical love and by the time they left Tom and Petra's they were in love again. Tom thought their behavior "cute" while Petra thought it a bit "bizarre" but of little consequence to her. And to Tom. They thought a little bit of intimacy was better than feuding. And their conversations over dinners were always bright, lively, and informative.

Their gettogethers and dinners were not regular, rather once every couple of months and at times spread even further apart. In the meantime Jim and Tom continued to write, sharing work with each other. They were, in effect, a mutal admiration society so there was never harsh criticism of one another or a conflict about who was the better writer. They supported each other.

These relationships continued over the years; things went well in a friendly way, Jim and Adrienne admiring and repecting Tom and Petra's solid and deep marriage, Tom and Petra amused by the ongoing disagreements, struggles, and reconciliations of their friends. At one point Jim, expressing his respect for Tom's writing and marriage, said that Tom was "a Jaguar in a world of Fords." Tom, surprised and pleased, but recognizing the hyperbole, responded with, "Yeah, on 15 cents worth of gas."

Then....

7/30/94—Jim and Adrienne have separated! A 'trial' separation. What a shock. Jim called to tell me and he was very calm about it. Petra and I saw them just two weeks ago and everything appeared normal (for them). Petra and I are amazed that we had no inkling that this was coming. So I, being a writer and always curious, made an attempt to find and evaluate causes and feelings and took a look back: I met Jim at Northport HS in 1969 just when he and Adrienne were getting together (both having been divorced). We watched them date, get married, raise their children by other spouses, lose Vicki, Jim's daughter, murdered at a bar where she got picked up by some low-life. It was a horror and we supported them through thick and thin.

When I first met Jim he was separated from Thelma and while divorcing her was living in a basement apartment that amounted to someone's cellar. It was very small, crowded and dismal. Upon meeting and developing a relationship with Adrienne, he moved into her house which she had acquired from her husband. And soon they married. On our visits there, we saw how Jim had turned the garage into a gym where he practised judo with determination and success. He was proud of his martial arts skills and demonstrated them to me. His emphasis on combat was strong and often, out of nowhere and with a wide grin, would tell me that his skill was so thorough that he could kill me "ten ways, nine of which are painful." Of course, it was not meant as a threat. It was an announcement of his success as an artist in judo.

As years went by they decided to sell the house and buy a condo and lo and behold some time later decided on a separation. I had picked up an unease in Jim but never this. The question is why? why? why? Jim says he's 'reality testing', can't see himself living his last 20 years this way. What way? What was wrong? Will they divorce? How little we really knew about their lives. True Jim and Adrienne have been a bit distant over the last year but we thought they were spreading out, looking for more active friends than Petra and I. That was okay with us—tennis and all that didn't interest us. Wrong. They've been seething and battling and here's the outcome—a separation.

8/4/94—Petra's been trying to get a hold of Adrienne. No go.

8/9/94—Adrienne returned the call and was immediately in tears. She is devastated. "How could this happen? After 18 years. I feel like I'm in a nightmare." She told us a lot but she held back a lot. "You don't know Jim. There are things I can't tell you." I assume other women; Petra suspects drugs. And maybe bisexuality. Who knows? There are paradoxes and ambiguities in all of us. Adrienne's still sleeping with Jim "when he spends the night." She bought him furniture for his new apartment, or helped him pick it out. She wants a legal separation but is afraid to bring it up. But she will, she says. She's trapped while trying to squeeze out of the mess he started. Apparently he thinks he can have it both ways. But what does he want? Nobody knows. Including Jim. Adrienne says she must start thinking about herself and her own life and interests. She's frantic and hurt but "as soon as I get off the phone I'm calling this guy I met." With tears in her voice no less. Petra's upset and I fear some violence. Adrienne says Jim wants to come out when we go to Montauk. Who wants to see him? To play games? And I think Adrienne is not aware of the contradictions in her own behavior, how she countenances what he does. A shrink told her she has destructive relationships with men. True? Bernie? Jim? Who's next for her to be the victim of? Petra can't figure either of them out. I'm tired of finding out that the people I know are not the people I know, that people, except those you really love, are masked. When you love, the masks are different, more lightweight, more dispensable, or the love comes before the mask, or the mask is for other aspects of your life not with the people you love....

8/12/94—Jim called, we talked for 45 minutes. The theme? He's free, free of marriage, free of constraints, free of guilt, free of convention, of being forced into a mold.

Epigraph: The core of the earth is on fire and so is the core of human beings.

8/14/94—So Jim is free. He sounds buoyant. He has no plans. He has no obligations. He's still fucking Adrienne but he doesn't love her anymore. He said sex and love are too much to handle together. He feels closer to himself. He likes living alone and writing, has contempt for the opinions of humanity, doesn't care what people say about him. He's free! If Adrienne finds someone, more power to her. If not, they'll be friends forever. "I care for her," he said. He gave her the larger share of the condo whatever they get when they sell it. He's at the gym five times a week. He looks great, he says. Adrienne's lost twenty pounds. He's in the Personals; so is Adrienne. They are both playing the field. Jim is enjoying it. He tells me I wouldn't survive living that kind of life. . "Anyway, keep Petra because she's a marvel. You have no idea what you'ver got there. You have a great relationship and a true marriage." He wants no particular woman; he's not on drugs; he's not leaving the area; he's simply free and will never marry again. He'll live alone very happily, free of women for whom he expressed great contempt.

8/19/94—We called Adrienne Friday night and got an hour's worth of it which contradicted most of what Jim told me last time. He's been banging a member of his own department, a 33 year old mother of a child, married to a well-off man she doesn't love. Jim tells Adrienne and she tells him to stop it. He stops it but the colleague keeps calling him. Adrienne accesses Jim's phone and that's all right with him. Adrienne says if the woman were in another district she wouldn't mind Jim fucking her, she could put up with it. But the fact that she's in the same school is humiliating. She is addicted to Jim, she says. Jim is on the phone many hours a day calling women. Adrienne is about to see a psychiatrist for anti-depressant drugs. She cries the whole time with her therapist. Jim says there are no rules so don't expect him to behave any particular way.

8/22/19—Adrienne called last night to tell us that she and Jim will not be coming to Montauk this year. "The whole thing is too fresh" for us to face each other. They are getting a legal separation and still fucking. Her shrink is working to get her off her "addiction" to Jim. She's on Prozac; he's on the telephone. So it goes.

10/7/94—Jim called. He sounded tense while trying to be his old self. Do I make him nervous? I asked to get together but he put me off. Forgot to get his new address so I left a message. We called Adrienne. No return call. He's off to Narcissista. Has he forced her to make the same trip? His textbook on history is selling pretty well. I figure he's made 8 grand so far. So I called the company and they seemed interested. I'll follow up.

10/14/94—Jim called. Read and commented positively on my novel. Had knee surgery, the quick kind. He's slowed down while Adrienne's speeded up. Wants to get together. Getting lonely, Jim?

10/18/94—Adrienne called and the tables are turned. Quite suddenly. She's free of Jim and meeting interesting men. She says Jim's depressed but she wants to be his friend. What happened to her addiction?

11/23/94—We called Adrienne. She's flying high because of Prozac, a shrink, and being pursued by at least three men. Sold the condo for less that they bought, is angry at Jim, is houseless, is the Girl of the Golden West to three men in their 40s and treating her like a queen. She doesn't think Jim is doing too well. I haven't heard from him.

12/1/94—Jim called, reported on my latest novel. He's cool, he belongs alone, he says. He's fine, Adrienne's fine, everybody's fine.

12/20/94—Call from Adrienne. She's flying high, has five boyfriends, is telling Jim off, is her own woman now, surrounded by admirers and a psychiatrist. She says Jim is unhappy. One ominous note—Jim is visiting Adrienne's daughter, calls her by mistake. Uh-oh. Watch out. The way to destroy Adrienne would be to fuck her daughter and ruin her marriage. I sent out a signal but Adrienne didn't pick it up.

4/10/95—Should write a short story about Jim and Adrienne and us. Won't it be familiar? How can I freshen it up? 1st person from me? Who's me? And Petra? Our stability? How little we humans know of each other.

5/11/95—Jim Eder called last night—late. Petra in bed doing better from her wrist operation but groggy from painkillers. Jim, ignoring her condition, brings me up to date. He's seeing someone; she's in her 30s, Jim's 55 and the "best shape ever"; wouldn't tell me her name, he's content he did the right thing, feels adult and autonomous for the first time in his life, is free, has moments (too much solitude and isolation), is moving from his tenement as he calls it into son's wife's apartment as they move on. Adrienne called, is networking, has all kinds of connections; one tragic one, a man she really loves, a fighter pilot in Vietnam, a psychologist who turned out to have an alcohol problem; she left him but got him into therapy but he died suddenly, age 46. Poor Adrienne. She's Pauline with her perils and bad luck with men. She and Jim are on and off. They fight then become civil. She says she'd never take him back now that she realizes how much shit she took from him. She's gotten her own condo, is still angry and hurt even though they always bragged that they had the best sex ever—always. He asked where we went in January (Tortola). He'd like to go but doesn't want to meet any "surly blacks." I told him about Greneda. He wanted to know how much. Wants to keep teaching til 60. It told him Petra and I will hit 40 years of marriage in July. He was impressed. "You two made it," he said. "You did it," "you had it."

7/11/95—Their divorce is settled. No hard feelings. Jim's happy. Adrienne's happy. Both have 'significant others'. Adrienne's under pressure at school not to show any grief or anger. She said "Jim's a bastard and I've wasted 20 years of my life on him. He's destroyed my love." She said she'll love someone again but never be *in love*, never be in a needy or subordinate role. Petra is suspicious of these distinctions.

8/2/95—Jim called. We talked somewhat warily at times. I have too many questions I can't ask and he's got too many realities he won't talk about. He's writing his memoirs now, his "sexual memoirs." Says his fiction was never very good. He's also writing a memoir about Vicki and wants me to read a couple of chapters. Meanwhile, he's "cool, detached, ready for anything, in great shape, slimmer than he has been in years, unfazed." After Vicky's murder and his divorce, he says he's been through the worst and quoting Nietzsche, "what doesn't kill me makes me stronger." He says he's maturer, wiser, while Adrienne calls him every black and derogatory name she can think of. He's completely in charge of his life, his "nomadic life," as he calls it; he's self-sufficient.

9/20/95—Funny how things change. I sent the whole of TEAVB to Jim and he sent me the chapters on Vicky. In correspondence, he blasted my book, actually hated it, said I should drop it, or at least make radical changes. I did not like what he wrote. Some of it was very coarse; other parts melodramatic. I liked the sarcasm about his first marriage but he was maudlin about him and Adrienne. Feeling as I did about the trauma over Vicki, I did not want to express all my criticism but my tone in the letter was cool.

5/7/96—So who calls? Adrienne. She's married. "You won't like him," she said outright. "I met him through the Personals. He's Bill, a lawyer. He's 47, this is a second marriage, no kids. He's not a big deal," she advised. "He loves me more that I love him and that's the way I want it. I'm never again going to love someone more than he loves me. He says I don't love him enough. I laugh." As for Jim, "He bought a house in N. and is living with Celia and her daughter. They're to be married soon. I'm happy. Don't I sound it? How's Petra? I thought of calling because someone at lunch mentioned blinds and I thought of Petra, so I'm calling. How's Jim? I've seen him once this year and that's it. How's he doing? You're asking me? I don't care."

How do I feel about Adrienne's call? That's a hard one. Petra said she has no feelings. Petra's indifferent because we never knew what was really going on when we thought we knew. She had warm feelings then. What value are her feelings now when nothing's authentic; when Adrienne may just be playing another game? So Petra's tuned them out. Is she feeling disappointment? Adrienne says blithely that she's happy but is Adrienne really happy? And Petra's amazed how quickly people shift their loyalties, their loves and affections, how quickly they recuperate after breakdowns. Is Adrienne still on Prozac? I didn't ask her. And she makes sure to call during the day, doesn't she? Is it so she doesn't have to confront or be confronted by Petra? Maybe I'm easier to talk to. She can handle me. I ask no embarrassing questions. But Petra wouldn't ask embarrassing questions either, but Adrienne knows Petra, she's observed her silences through it all and maybe she feels Petra's silences are judgments.

So how do I feel?

*

Five years later Tom got a letter from Jim:

"Tom, I got your synopses. I don't understand why you continue to send your stuff to me. Since Adrienne and I are finished, it's be obvious to me that you harbor some resentment against me. Because you've always been a fair-minded guy, I figure it was more than some judgment about the divorce. I learned to cope with the things Adrienne said about me to colleagues, neighbors, friends, even classes of students. I lived my life and tried to keep my dignity while knowing that people who hardly knew me thought they knew all about me.

"I expected more of you. I would have respected you if you had either confronted me or ignored me all together. At this point, I'm more comfortable with the latter. Jim."

Some time later I had a dream in which Jim arrived dressed in a blue suit (light, dark tie). He had a manuscript which he threw at me. Then we were working together on it. This time he was wearing a black jacket. As we conferred, he opened a window and threw some papers out. One was a newspaper with a headline that read, "I didn't kill her. I didn't kill my wife."

*

12/1/2009: I was told Jim died. He was 69. No response from Petra who has been diagnosed with Alzheimer's disease. That diagnosis consumes us.

Chapter Twenty-Five

Well before Tom and Petra moved out Tom applied his time-honored technique of bringing down dead tree branches. He tied a rope around half a brick, determined the height of the branch and heaved the brick over it. Holding onto the end of the rope Tom watched as the rope snaked up and grew taut as the brick came down with a thud on the other side of the target, a high dead branch. He picked up the brick, moved out from under the branch and, taking a deep breath, yanked hard at the rope. He heard a crack. He yanked again. Another crack. After a third try the branch fell and broke into piece on the lawn not feet form him.

While he was performing his preferred method a van came up the driveway. It was the pool company guys. The men he had seen a day or so before now continued measuring the ground and marking trees with red spray paint.

"That tree's coming down," one of them men said as he watched Tom heave the brick over another dead branch.

"Is it?" Tom said.

"Yeah," the young man said, "and that one and that one."

"I planted them," Tom said, "I planted evey single bush and tree and flower bed on my property. This was all barren twenty years ago."

"You did a nice job."

"Well, I overdid it a little, overplanted like any city dweller looking for a touch of nature for himself."

"It's nice here," the older man said.

"We love trees," Tom said, "and you should have seen those azaleas over there when they flowered."

"Those have to go, too," the young man said.

"They still have to be pruned. We've got time yet."

"Those trees and everything will be gone soon," the young man said.

"They still have to be trimmed," Tom said.

"It's a big pool they're putting in."

"I know. These people are pool-happy. Give me the trees. They were all this high when I put them in."

Tom leveled his hand at his shoulder.

"Now look at them," the older man said. "You can't beat nature."

They continued marking trees for destruction.

After cleaning up the broken branches, Tom went about transplanting pachysandra, taking plants from a crowded bed and filling in a thin one.

"Look at him," the young man said quietly. "He's right in the middle of the pool."

"Leave'im alone," the older man said. "He knows where the pool is going."

*

"Don't be silly," Petra said when she came home from shopping and found her husband on his hands and knees. "Tom, this is all a wasted effort. You should be calling the real estate people instead. Come and help me with the packages."

He walked to the car with dirty hands. The knees of his blue jeans were smudged with dark soil and damp.

"Did you get hold of Jim?" Petra asked. "Did he get the results of the engineer's report yet?"

"I didn't call."

"Why not? Please don't leave me with everything to do."

Tom stopped in the middle of the kitchen with a package in his hands.

"That engineer gave me one of the worst days in my life."

"Why?" Petra asked. "Did he find something major?"

"No. It wasn't that. It was his detachment and objectivity. I hated it."

"How long was he here?"

"Over an hour. It was an ordeal. I didn't know what to do with myself. It was like waiting for the doctor to tell me if I had cancer or not."

"Oh, don't be so dramatic," Petra said, taking the package from him. "It's only a house he's inspecting."

"Ours," Tom said. "He went from room to room with his searchlight and his clipboard making his little notes and inding fault."

"Don't take it personally. It's his job. We'll have to hire one ourselves when we find what we want."

Tom wasn't listening.

"He practically crawled on his knees through the basement and around the foundation, he went up the attic, checked all the plumbing, all the outlets and let me know every little problem."

"It's his job."

"He never once said how nice the house looked."

"Oh, Tom, really, what did you expect from the man?"

"I felt like I was being judged."

"Whatever he finds wrong we'll fix," Petra said. "That's all. Let's just hope there's nothing major."

"There's nothing major," Tom said. "We know what this house is worth."

"Then relax."

"I can't stand that cold objectivity so I went out and started taking down some dead branches."

"What for?" Petra said. "Those trees are coming down."

"I just felt like it."

"You and that brick of yours. You're going to hurt yourself with that brick and I'm not paying for a tree surgeon."

"It's my tried and true method. I've been very comfortable here," Tom said.

"And so have I," Petra said, "and now it's time to move on."

"I know. There are some branches I can't reach. I hate to see dead branches in trees."

"We'll be gone soon."

"And then the pool men came and marked the trees. Do they have to take all of them down?"

"On that side. It's a pool. Just forget about it."

"I'll forget about it soon enough," Tom said.

"Then don't waste your time and energy. You'll bop yourself with that brick one of thse days and then we'll be in trouble."

"It's spring," Tom said. "It has to be done."

He paused at the door before going out.

"You know what the engineer said to me? When he finished the inspection he came up to me and said, 'No house is perfect.'"

"He probably saw the look on your face."

"That's a hell of a job. Going into people's homes and telling them what's wrong with it."

"It's got to be done."

"And so does the pruning," Tom said.

"But the trees are coming down, Tom."

"That's a terrible thing to live with," was Tom's response.

"What is?"

"To find fault with every house you walk into."

"It's his job."

"I can't tell you how I felt all day," Tom said. "So I transplanted some pachysandra."

"That's going, too," Petra said appeasingly.

"I never want to come back here."

"You don't have to. We'll have a new home."

"I've been very comfortable here."

He walked out and was soon counting all the trees slashed with red paint.

CPSIA information can be obtained
at www.ICGtesting.com
Printed in the USA
LVHW010504180720
661005LV00002B/126